NOBODY'S DOG

For Emily, who doesn't like dogs and would have torn up the typescript

NOBODY'S DOG

Grace Griffiths

A TARGET BOOK
published by
the Paperback Division of
W. H. ALLEN & CO. PLC

A Target Book
Published in 1986
By the Paperback Division of
W. H. Allen & Co. PLC
44 Hill Street, London W1X 8LB

Printed and bound in Great Britain by
Anchor Brendon Ltd, Tiptree, Essex

ISBN 0 426 20250 3

Chapter One

'We'll have to get rid of him,' said the woman.

'Well, he's your dog. It's up to you,' replied the man as he stumped off into the garden.

The dachshund puppy cowered under the kitchen table. Once again he had offended these difficult human beings.

The woman had bought him from a pet shop when he was only eight weeks old. He remembered the shop very clearly. The owner smelled of stale food, but the hutches in which the pets were kept were very clean. The dog had shared a pen with three terrier puppies. Beside them was a cage of kittens, and ranged along the opposite wall were hamsters, gerbils, rabbits and white mice. On the counter was a hutch containing some guinea-pigs, and above them hung a mynah bird in a cage. Every time the doorbell pinged as a customer entered the bird said, 'Hello,' and when the same bell gave a sort of strangled hiccup, which meant that the customer was going out of the shop, the bird said, 'Goodbye-come-again-soon-won't-you?' in one breathless sentence.

Life in the pet shop was interesting. The owner was generous with food, and most of the customers spared a moment to run their fingers up and down the bars of the cage or to scratch the puppies' noses. The kittens and gerbils were always playing games and tumbling over each other, and when a lady took away two of the little cats leaving only a tortoiseshell female, the puppies felt that they had lost some friends. The remaining kitten had cried piteously when she found that she was all alone and the puppies had barked in sympathy. The mynah bird had become so upset by the noise that he called, 'Hello,' to a customer leaving the shop and had said, 'Goodbye,' to someone who was entering. The hamsters had hidden themselves under their wood shavings so that the cage appeared to be empty, and the grey doe rabbit tucked herself away in the far corner of her hutch. Only the mice on their treadmill seemed unaffected by the uproar. Their tiny pink paws continued to scrabble on the wheel, their shell-pink ears remained pricked, their noses twitched and their eyes shone. But the noise made by the puppies and the kitten had upset the owner who cried, 'What am I to do? My shop is like a madhouse,' and he went from cage to cage talking to the animals and quietening them with tit-bits. At last the kitten went to sleep, and the puppies fell over themselves playing with a rubber ball, but the mynah bird continued to jump up and down on his perch saying, 'Hello-goodbye-come-again-soon-won't-you-hello . . .'

It was not long after this mishap that the woman bought the dachshund. She had taken him home in a shopping basket covered by a waterproof cover, and in her kitchen she had given him chopped meat, biscuits and a bowl of milk.

The house was on the outskirts of the town. Traffic rumbled ceaselessly past the front door, but at the back there was a garden with an apple tree. At first the puppy had stayed indoors, and his mistress had pampered him. After a few days she had taken him into the garden and left him to romp among the young plants. When he had grown older she had put a collar around his neck and taken him for walks along the street. He quickly learned that as long as he stayed on the pavement he was safe from the noisy lorries and cars which dashed along the roadway.

He had grown rapidly, his coat becoming sleek and smooth, his ears broad and silky and his nose black and moist. 'Beautiful Hans. Hans is a beautiful boy,' cooed his mistress as he lay on her lap, but, 'Naughty Hans. Wicked, wicked dog,' she shouted when his long claws snagged her nylon tights. His master too, was angry when he dug up the lettuces in the garden or broke down the young bean plants. 'Beastly, horrible dog,' they cried when his adult teeth began to come through his gums and he felt that he must chew things to ease the soreness in his mouth. He had splintered the leg of a kitchen chair and completely destroyed a photograph album which had been left lying on the coffee table, torn all the fur trimming from his mistress's slippers and eaten the middle pages of a library book. At first they had slapped him, then they had beaten him with a cane, but he had never been quite sure why.

After he had pulled a newly washed nightdress from the clothesline and worried it until it was almost split in two, they had beaten him and shut him in an outhouse, but he had quickly escaped by digging a tunnel under the wooden walls. Not wanting to be beaten again he had run into the next door garden where he had chased the family cat, an aged and arthritic tom, up a cherry tree. He had finally been returned to his owners by a loudly complaining neighbour.

He was no longer trusted to go into the garden alone, so when his people went out he was shut in the kitchen. But from the moment that he heard the front door click shut and realised that he was alone, he complained loudly. At first he yapped, a shrill, piercing, high-pitched yap, then he whined, and when no-one came, he howled. The neighbours on both sides were annoyed, and once more he was beaten. He felt miserable and rebellious, and no longer tried to please his owners or to be clean in the house. He left puddles on the carpets and was sick on the stairs. No-one petted him. No-one said, 'Hans is a beautiful boy.' He was 'that dog' or 'that little beast'.

'I can't stand it any longer,' cried the woman. 'He'll have to go. We've got to get rid of him.'

'Well, he's your dog,' replied the man. 'It's up to you.'

Later they talked about the market and the RSPCA. Finally they agreed to put an advertisement in the local paper offering him free to a good home. 'I want him out of here by the weekend,' said the woman.

Days passed. Two ladies came to the house asking about the young dachshund which was to be given away, but he snarled at one because she stroked his back where it hurt from his last beating, and the other lady saw a puddle in the hall and said, 'But he's not house-trained! And you say he's already four months old.'

'No-one will have him,' cried the woman. 'What can we do?'

'I'll take him to the RSPCA,' answered the man, and he went off to fetch the car.

Hans was put on the back seat. The leather covering was worn and scuffed. On the way to the centre of the town the little dog managed to rip the fabric right across, but the man was concentrating on his driving and did not notice. It was not until they reached the RSPCA dispensary that he saw the damage, and then he was furious. He hit the puppy hard and shook him until his teeth rattled, then he tucked him under his arm and strode towards the building. But the time was 6.15 pm and a notice on the door said that the place closed at 6 pm. The man swore. Once more he flung the dachshund onto the back seat and drove off, taking the road which led out of the town. The little dog lay with his chin on his paws and sighed, watching the man sideways. He knew that he had offended again.

Outside the town the man took the turning

which led to the motorway. The September sun was still high in the sky and the air coming through the windows of the car was soft and warm. The dachshund smelled unfamiliar country smells – mown grass, fresh-turned earth, cows and the pungent smell of horses. His nostrils twitched and his eyes swivelled from side to side, but he did not dare move.

The car sped down the motorway. Other traffic thundered past, overtaking, their slipstreams causing the car to rock. At times the noise was deafening.

After a while the man pulled over to the hard shoulder and drew to a stop. For a moment there was no other vehicle in sight. He opened the passenger door, and said, 'Out, Hans! Go! Scat!' The dog scrambled out, mystified at this unexpected invitation to freedom, and then as he sniffed at the bushes by the roadside, the man flung his car into gear and drove off.

At first the animal was pleased to find himself free and alone. The hedge was full of enticing smells, so he wandered along the verge of the motorway investigating a scent here, savouring a scent there. From his walks in the busy streets near his home he knew all about cars, and he had sense enough to keep out of their path, but he did not leave the roadside. The fields which stretched away behind the hedge, with their tall grasses and neat rows of crops, were strange territory to him which he did not want to investigate.

Soon the bushes gave way to a low, stone wall

which ran along the edge of the road for several hundred yards. It was not as interesting as the hedge, and the young dog grew bored. Across the motorway a grassy strip continued, backed by patches of brambles and gorse bushes. He paused and sniffed the air and looked cautiously left and right. The road was clear. He darted across all three lanes to the central division and there he stopped. Again he tested the air and cocked his ears. A car was coming from the right, but it was still a long way off. He trotted diagonally across the first lane and then paused for a moment for the road seemed to shake and a thunderous noise was almost upon him.

Panic swept over him and he bolted for the far side. There was a long drawn out squeal of brakes and a crash of metal on metal followed by human screams and a smell of burning. The little dachshund flattened his ears and dived for the safety of the verge: behind him a small car was burning furiously beneath a heavy truck which had cannoned into it as its driver braked to avoid the dog. But the dachshund neither knew nor cared. Still terrified by the noise of the accident he scurried across the grass verge and scrambled through the hedge leaving behind him the frightening ways of humans and all the things he had learned to fear and hate.

Chapter Two

The field which he was crossing sloped down to a brook where cows were drinking. These were strange animals so he approached them warily, but he was thirsty and the only place where the stream ran shallowly between low banks was where the cows were gathered. The warm wet smell of the animals came to him on the summer breeze where he lay flattened in the grass. His nostrils twitched: the smell was strangely comforting; it reminded him of his mother's milk and the security of the place where she had suckled him together with his brothers and sisters. He lay and watched, and after a while he crept forward, stomach to the ground, dodging between the black and white legs of the strange beasts. As he neared the water one of the cows bent her head and made as if to toss him, while her hooves slipped in the mud along the edge of the stream. The other animals bunched together and wheeled so that the dog found himself on the fringe of a hostile circle. He paused, ears drooping dolefully, tail tucked between his legs, eyes alert. The cow nearest to him mooed, a harsh throat-tearing sound. It was too much: the dog turned and fled, while the cows watched, flicking their tails in unison, their soft brown eyes full of curiosity. To the dachshund they were a terrifying sight.

He did not stop running until he reached the hedge which bordered the pasture. There he turned and uttered a shrill, defiant yap at his distant enemies.

The hedge was riddled with rabbit burrows, and the young dog quickly forgot his thirst as he explored the exciting scents which clung to the brambles and clumps of nettles, but soon he was again near the stream and this time he drank his fill. He stood ankle-deep in the cool water and lapped until the froth accumulated on his lower jaw and his stomach was so distended that it almost touched the surface of the brook. Splashing flat-footedly, he clambered onto dry land and lay in the sunshine: presently he slept.

When he awoke, shadows from the hedge were creeping over the field and a cool breeze blew drifts of buttercup pollen across the grasses. The little dog felt hungry and he set off in a confused sort of way for home and supper, but very soon he realised that he was lost. He crossed field after field, scrambling through hedges and crawling through patches of gorse and bracken. Once he came to a marsh and splashed his way through mud and water, trampling rushes and lady's smock, until he reached dry ground. It was growing dark and a faint mist hung over the surface of the grass. On all sides there were rustlings and strange noises which terrified him. He ran blindly, his low-slung body coated with mud, and his ears and tail thick with burrs and the green seedballs of goose-grass. He ran with his muzzle stretched forwards and his tail tucked between his back legs. Occasionally he paused to listen: he was very, very frightened.

When he could run no longer he crept into a patch of nettles and lay there panting. An owl hooted a long way off.

Exhausted, he slept fitfully, troubled by the strange noises around him. When he awoke the moon was riding high. The nettles were deep in the shadow of the hedge but the rest of the field was as bright as day. The grasses were full of stealthy movement. In the distance the anguished scream of a rabbit, cornered by a weasel, rang out through the night. The dachshund trembled and kept very still in his hiding-place: fear made him forget how cold and hungry he was.

The long night passed slowly. Towards dawn, a hare, returning to her form, leaped suddenly over the dog who gave a low moan of terror and flattened himself against the ground.

As soon as it was light he crept from his resting-place and set off once more. Hunger flooded his consciousness, and he ran as fast as his short legs would carry him. His paws left dark prints on the dew-silvered grass.

Gradually the sun rose and its warmth dried the ground. Daisies opened pink-tipped petals, and purple foxgloves stood tall in the hedgerows. Butterflies fluttered vaguely from flower to flower and bumble bees plunged deep into every blossom

14

in search of nectar. The soothing sounds of the day together with the weakness he felt from lack of food caused the young dog to slacken his pace, and soon he was trotting gently, pausing now and again to sniff a new smell or to rest in the shade of a bush.

It was almost noon when he came to the harvest field. The sun rode high in the blue arch of the sky and the heat was intense. A group of farm workers who had been harvesting a field of wheat were sitting in the shade of a hedge eating their mid-day snack when the dog came upon them. The smell of meat sandwiches overcame his fear of strangers, and he slumped, panting, tongue hanging out beside the youngest labourer. At first he begged with his eyes, then he made little whimpering sounds in his throat and poked the man's leg with his paw until a piece of bread was broken off and thrown to him. He snapped it up ravenously.

'Famished, I reckon,' said one of the older men.

'And lost too,' muttered another. 'Look at his coat; all mud and dashels.'

'He's naught but a baby,' cried the youngest man. 'Can't look after hisself.'

They gave him all they could spare, but to the dachshund it seemed little enough. When they went back to work he slept curled up on the young man's jacket.

Later that afternoon when the grain was all harvested, the men came to collect their luncheon satchels from the hedge. The dog was dozing, head resting on his front paws, watching the men through half-closed eyes. He thumped his tail on the ground when the owner of the jacket approached.

'Come on then, Bob, me boyo,' cried his new friend, snapping his fingers. 'You'd better come home along with me.'

The dachshund rose and trotted after him. They crossed three fields and went up a lane to a small farm cottage. At the door the man called, 'Hey, Mary, look at this.' His wife, a plump rosy-cheeked girl bustled out.

'Oh, the poor lamb! Let me 'ave 'n, Bill. Lor what a mess 'ees in.'

In no time at all she had combed the burrs from his coat and brushed out the hair which was tangled with mud. Then she gave him a bowl of meat and vegetables covered with delicious gravy. The dog ate his fill and then slunk under the kitchen table where he lay, sighing his contentment. The woman lined an empty potato box with an old woollen skirt and put it by the window. Presently the dachshund crept into it and slept.

Chapter Three

Autumn turned to early winter. The dachshund, cossetted and well-fed by his new friends, grew sleek and strong. 'No wonder they calls 'un sausage dog,' mused the man. ''E's just a lil' ole bit of 'og's pudden on legs.'

'Doan' ee laugh at 'un,' answered his wife, ''e's just as God made 'un and no mistake. Just as you be.'

In truth, he *was* a beautiful animal. His dense chocolate-brown coat shone from frequent groomings, his skin moved loosely and supplely over his frame, his eyes shone and his nose was cool and moist. His short strong forelegs were slightly crooked as in all of his kind, and his front paws, with their long black claws, were splayed outwards. He had a long low muscular body, but he carried his head high, boldly and defiantly; his expression was at once both enquiring and intelligent. The woman loved to play with his broad silky ears and to tickle his nose with a chicken feather until he sneezed and ran off only to come back later to be teased and fondled again. She taught him to sit up on his hind quarters to beg for food and tried to teach him to balance a ball on his nose, but this his dignity forbade.

The farmer, on whose land the cottage stood, was not pleased that his workman had adopted a dog. Sheepdogs he liked and admired, but an animal which did not work seemed to him an unnecessary luxury. 'Keep 'n away from the sheep,' he warned the man, but the dog left all the farm animals alone.

From time to time his new master took him rabbiting. It was a sport which the dachshund quickly came to enjoy for his forebears had been trained as badger hunters for generations. Age-old instincts came into play as he scampered down a burrow to frighten the inhabitants out into the open where the man had spread nets over all the exits from the warren. He gambolled with pleasure and excitement as the terrified animals tried to escape from the meshes which entrapped them. The same instincts taught him to slide through a low passage on his broad, strong chest, his front feet stretched out before him so the depth of the hole was no obstacle to him.

The other farm workers marvelled at the number of rabbits which the young man could send to the local market and could not understand why their own mongrels were not as quick to find and seek out the prey. The little dog loved the work, and his master had only to rise from his chair to take the nets which hung behind the kitchen door for the dachshund to bark excitedly and to run to the door, his eyes shining with excitement and anticipation. Often it was he who would choose the bank where they would work, sniffing the ground and scrabbling with his paws but never barking, because now the hunt was on.

Once when he entered a burrow he came face to face with a stoat which was also hunting rabbits. Both animals stood motionless facing each other. The stoat, the smaller of the two, knew that he had the advantage of plenty of room in which to manoeuvre while the dog could only advance or wriggle out backwards from the narrow passage-way. The dachshund had never seen a stoat at close quarters before, but he recognized the menace in the slim, sinuous body and the angry, red eyes which confronted him. His hackles rose and he tensed himself for a fight perhaps to the death. The muscles on his shoulders rippled smoothly as he planted his forelegs wide. Neither animal moved but their gaze locked in a long, threatening stare. Then, without any warning, the stoat hurled itself at the dog's throat. The dachshund thrust him aside with his muzzle although the rapier teeth of his enemy raked his cheek. The stoat sprang again, and this time the dog snapped at him in mid-air and caught a foreleg between his jaws. The wounded animal fell back, his eyes bloodshot with fury; the pain in his leg was agonizing, but with the mindless courage of his kind he would fight on. Equally, the dog, brave and stubborn as are all his breed, had no thought of retreat although blood was pouring from his gashed cheek. Once more they clashed, but this time the stoat was hampered by his injured leg. He fell easy prey to the dog which seized his whole head in his jaws and crushed it as he would crush a chicken bone. Only then did he wriggle backwards out of the burrow dragging his dead enemy with him.

The man was amazed when he realised what had happened for he knew the stoat to be a vicious and determined killer, able to defeat an enemy twice his size by the speed of his attack, the needle-sharpness of his teeth and the unbridled fury of his assault. He knew that the dog, confined in the narrow burrow, would have been at a grave dis-advantage, and he marvelled at the dachshund's courage and determination. He pressed together the edges of the tear on the little dog's cheek so that it ceased to bleed, and he threw the mangled body of the stoat into a ditch. Within a few minutes the dachshund was asking to go into the burrow again.

That evening they made a record catch of rabbits, and the dog swaggered into the cottage with a new self-importance. It was as though the fight with the stoat, followed by his outstanding success in the hunt, had proved his maturity.

The weather grew colder and snow lay thick on the ground so that for some weeks there was no rabbiting. In the cottage the kitchen was warmed by a sweet smelling log fire which burned on the hearth. The dog, restless from lack of exercise roamed the farmyard by day and slept in the potato box at night. Gradually the snow cleared but a warm westerly wind brought storms of tor-rential rain. The garden became a morass, the farmyard a mire, and the man returned from his work in the fields soaked to the skin in spite of the heavy clothing in which he was clad. When the days began to lengthen the storms blew themselves out and for several days there was no wind at all. The days were bright and cold; the nights were rimed with frost. Each morning the golden orb of the sun rose in a pallid sky, but in those yellow dawns no bird sang. An eerie silence filled the windless spell and hung heavily on the leafless trees, and the garden was winter-bare of flowers. 'It's not natural,' said the man, 'everything's much too quiet.' In the evenings he watched the moon rise in the starlit sky, and shook his head. Something was wrong: the dog felt his uneasiness.

Suddenly the weather broke. Great masses of cloud built up in the west, and a fitful wind gusted across the fields. A distant rumble of thunder came nearer and grew louder. The sky was riven by forked lightning. The jagged outline of the moors loomed stark and black on the horizon, and the winter wheat shivered, its young greenness shadowed with grey in the half-light. Rain fell in sheets, flooding down the cottage chimney and extinguishing the fire, finding weak places in the thatch of the roof and soaking into the bedroom ceilings. The garden path became a stream which was quickly dammed by leaves and gravel so that water flowed in under the front door.

The first flash of lightning had so frightened the dog that he had run upstairs and hidden under the bed, and there he stayed until the storm abated.

Neither the man nor the woman paid him any attention for they were far too busy trying to cope with the damage to their home.

When at last the weather eased and the thunder had rumbled away into the distance, the dachshund came out to find his master and mistress in great distress. Part of the roof had been torn away, the ceilings in the bedrooms were sagging and the kitchen floor was covered by a thick film of mud.

Later the farmer came to look at his property and promised to send men to do the necessary repairs as soon as possible, but the woman said that she would not spend another winter in the cottage, come what may. She reminded her husband that nowadays farmers usually provided well-built, modern cottages for their men and said that although she was country born and bred she had never thought to live in a pigsty.

It was lambing time and the man was often called out to help at night, but he was told that on no account was he to bring the dog with him because the farmer thought that it might frighten the ewes. This made the woman very impatient for she was sure that the dachshund would never trouble the sheep. She kept saying what a bad boss the farmer made and telling her husband that he should seek work elsewhere, but the man said little. After the farmhand had gone out, the animal howled dismally and scrabbled at the bottom of the door, nor could the woman comfort him. When the labourer returned, tired and muddy and smelling of sheep, the dog greeted him with shining eyes and lashing tail.

Slowly the weather grew warmer; primroses sprinkled the hedgerows and there were daffodils in the woods. Lambing time was over, the cottage was mended and once more neat and clean, but the woman still complained. Why could they not live nearer a town in a nice little modern house, she asked.

In early June when the cherry tree in the corner of the garden was drifting its pale petals to the ground, she started to pack clothes and kitchen utensils in large boxes. The dachshund grew tired of watching her and ran off into the fields to follow the scents which lay among the grasses. The sun was hot on his back and he had a long and pleasurable day moving farther and farther away from the cottage. He went further than he had ever gone before, and at sunset he was circling a church in a small village some two miles from the farm. He was not hungry because he had eaten some scraps which he had found in a garden and had drunk some milk which had been put out for a cat. The sense of adventure was strong upon him, and he did not want to leave this new and exciting place until he had explored it properly. He ran across the churchyard and came to a street of shops and houses. A man was reversing a car into a garage while a cat sat watching. She saw the dog almost as soon as he saw her, and she arched her body and spat. The dachshund halted, and then with a quiver of delight, rushed towards his new playmate, remembering dimly the smell of cat from his days in the pet shop, but as the animal shot away she roused his instinct to chase and he sped after her. She fled into the garage followed by the dog, and then she flew under the car and out through the still open door. The dachshund, momentarily puzzled, skidded to a halt behind the vehicle, and in that moment the man shut and locked the garage door.

It was a few minutes before the dog realised that he was trapped. Then he scratched the door and barked until he found that no-one would let him out: finally, he curled up on a pile of sacks and slept.

Chapter Four

The man did not use his car again for almost a week. As the dachshund grew hungrier and more frightened he howled and barked and scrabbled at the garage door, but no-one heard him, no-one came to let him out. A bucket half filled with water provided him with the means to quench his thirst, but he found nothing to eat at all. His coat grew lank and staring, and he lost so much weight that his hip bones and ribs stood out in ridges on his body. On the sixth day he heard steps outside the garage door and he summoned all his strength to bark as loudly as he possibly could. The door opened. The dog wasted no time on the astonished man who stood there, but shot past him as fast as his legs would carry him and was away over the fields to home.

He bounded along, ears flapping and tail streaming out behind him with never a thought for the creatures he passed on the way. No strange smells enticed him: he was blind and deaf to everything, filled with the consuming desire to reach the cottage and food as soon as possible. A group of crows scavenging in a hayfield took wing noisily as he passed: a tabby cat crouched before a rabbit hole lost her nerve and fled up an alder tree when she saw the lithe brown body hurtling towards her. The stench of her fear did not even tickle his nostrils. His breath came in snorts and his legs felt weak, but his need to reach home gave him the strength to run on.

When he reached the cottage it seemed strangely silent. The doors and windows were closed, and he could hear no movement within. He scratched at the door and barked and jumped up and rattled the handle, but no-one came. When he climbed onto the window-ledge he saw that the kitchen was bare. Lying on his stomach on the front door step he howled and howled . . .

The day wore on. Soon the need for food drove him to the farmyard where he found some scraps and a saucer of milk which had been put out for the farm cats. He wolfed all this as well as some mash which he found in the chicken trough and this indigestible but filling meal made him feel a lot happier and stronger. When he had satisfied himself that there was no more food to be found in the yard, he went back to the cottage to sleep in the shade of the cherry tree.

At sunset he awoke and scratched at the cottage door again but he knew in his heart that no-one would come: the smell of the man and his wife was very faint and stale. He could not understand why they had deserted him and he was filled with an awful sense of desolation: they were *his* people, surely they would come back. But all the signs showed that they had gone forever. When the moon rose into the milky sky, he howled until, exhausted, he crept into the outhouse and slept.

He stayed near the cottage for several days, seeking his food in the farmyard and sleeping wherever he found a comfortable spot. Sometimes, a little hopelessly, he barked or howled at the door; sometimes he hung around the farmhouse only to be cursed and chased away when the farmer saw him. The food which he found was meagre and not very nourishing and he grew thinner and thinner, but he was afraid to leave his old home in case the man and his wife came back.

Then one afternoon when he was stretching and shaking the sleep from his eyes after his noonday nap, a truck drove up to the cottage door and a man started to unload furniture. A woman climbed wearily from the passenger seat and went into the house. Surely she must be a friend, he thought, and he followed her into the cottage, but when she saw him, she shuddered away and the man came and shooed him out. After that he lay in the long grass at the end of the garden and watched as tables, chairs, crates of china and bedding were carried indoors.

Finally the truck rumbled away and the door of the house was closed. Once more he started to howl, but the new tenants of the cottage came and threw stones at him until he ran to hide in the farmyard. It was obvious that they did not like dogs, but he was loath to leave the place where he had known so much happiness and comfort. When he tried to slip through the front door, the woman shouted at him and the man used his boot.

The farmer told the man that the dog had belonged to his former employee who had had to leave him behind because he had gone missing on their removal day. 'Don't bother with 'un. Ef 'ee's a nuisance, why don't 'ee shoot 'un?'

'That I might,' replied the man, and the next time the dachshund howled, a charge of small shot whistled over his head, some of the pellets lodging in his ears. The dog knew about guns and he realised that the man meant business. He did not stay any longer, but ran off to lie shivering on the other side of a hedge. When night fell he slunk away and went south. The shot in his ears was just beneath the skin and every movement made the wounds smart. He was still puzzled about why his people had deserted him and he was filled with misery and a deep distrust of all human beings.

He avoided the village where he had been shut in the garage and followed the course of a stream upwards towards the moor. He travelled throughout the whole night and slept at dawn. On the following afternoon he continued his journey toward the high moors, only stopping to beg food at moorland cottages. His ears were beginning to fester; one woman tried to bathe them while he ate, but he snarled at her and snapped at her hands. He was no longer the sleek, supple creature who had lived with the labourer and his wife. Misery had shortened his temper, his coat was rough and patched with mud, his black eyes were sunken and lifeless, his paws were swollen and torn and his ears were dark with dried blood. For several days he travelled upwards, drinking from streams, cadging food wherever he could, catching sometimes a young rabbit. His thin body grew hard with muscle: the wounds in his ears suppurated and the small shot was thrown out. Blowflies laid eggs on the dried pus and their maggots cleaned the sores so that they healed healthily.

When he reached the high moors he was forced to live entirely on the voles, rats and small mammals that he could catch for himself. Until the yellowing bracken told of the coming of autumn, he roamed the highland, sleeping in holes in the rocks, running across the desolate heathland by day, a tiny, solitary figure against the backdrop of the tors.

As the nights grew longer and colder he longed for the comfort of the cottage. At first the bitter moorland winds raked his small body, but gradually, very gradually, his coat thickened and he no longer felt the cold.

One night he sought shelter among the stones of a ruined hut circle where he was amazed to find a strong scent of dog upon the granite. He sniffed from rock to rock, following the scent of not one dog but several. His hackles rose, and a low growl broke from his throat. Around him in the gathering darkness, eyes, tiny points of light, were watching him: he was encircled. To show goodwill and submission he lay down and put his head on his paws, swishing his tail gently, while first one dog and then another came forward to sniff at him. He growled quietly, a small token of protest and snapped half-heartedly at an Alsatian which brought its muzzle a little too near. The bigger dog snarled and snapped back, and in no time at all the dachshund was fighting for his life. His enemy, who was much bigger and stronger than he was, repeatedly bowled him over and tore his ears and shoulders with his sharp teeth. But the little dog was small enough to roll between his opponent's paws and he had the advantage of speed. The other dogs, a couple of mongrels, a collie bitch, a greyhound cross and a pair of sheepdogs, sat in a circle and watched.

When the dachshund no longer had the strength to roll himself free from the Alsatian, he lay flat, blood pouring from wounds on his neck and sides, while the other dog worried him. Then, quite suddenly, the fight was over: his opponent moved off and the collie came forward to lick his ears and flanks. The Alsatian, a huge, black beast with white paws, had established his superiority, and the dachshund was now accepted into the pack.

He stayed with the wild dogs, sharing their food and sleeping in their den. By day they kept under cover, but at night they searched the moor for food. The collie, the Alsatian and the sheepdogs, all shepherds by instinct, loved to harry and round up the moorland sheep. Followed by the dachshund and the mongrels and outstripped by the greyhound, they would circle a grazing flock, sinking on their stomachs and watching the unwary animals until, as if at a prearranged signal, they moved forwards forcing the milling sheep to run in this direction or that. The shepherd dogs moved quietly, the greyhound bounded around at a distance, the mongrels hung around on the outskirts while the dachshund panted up in the rear. The bleating flock was sent off down the hillside with the dogs snapping at the heels of the hindmost. Often the greyhound streaked ahead so that the sheep were suddenly confronted by him and did not know which way to turn. Blind with panic they scrambled between rocks and bushes and quickly became scattered over the moor. Sometimes they fled into a swiftly running stream and the old and the weak were drowned. Sometimes a terrified animal slipped among the rocks and broke a leg. A damaged beast was fair game to the wild pack which tore the meat from her living body, while hungry crows circled overhead. All the dogs ate the meat. Even the dachshund took his share.

Chapter Five

It was a long hard winter on the hills. From early December an icy wind seared the uplands. At night the bracken was encrusted with frost, and although the sun rose daily into a cloudless sky, its warmth was not enough to melt the ice. The rocky ground felt harder than ever beneath the dogs' feet, and they were able to cross bogs and mires as if they were dry land. They slept huddled together for warmth with the little dachshund somewhere in the middle of the tangle of shaggy bodies. The black Alsatian led the pack well, finding water for them in streams that ran too fast to freeze over, or cracking ice so that they could reach the unfrozen water underneath. He found food too, leading them to animals which were dying from lack of food or to warrens where rabbits briefly played outside. Sometimes the dachshund entered the burrows to flush out the prey, and his skill in doing this was recognized by the other dogs.

At the year's end snow fell and a blizzard which lasted several weeks blanketed the hills in whiteness. Now there was no shortage of water for the pack since they licked up the snow itself, but food was very scarce. The supply of small mammals which could be tracked across the snow-covered waste was limited and sometimes the dogs could only find birds which had fallen from the air half-dead from cold and starvation. After a few weeks nothing stirred on the desolate hills. Most of the sheep had been driven into folds by the farmers when the bad weather began: the few that remained were buried deep in snowdrifts between the rocks. In the long cold nights and icy days the wild dogs grew hungrier and hungrier. They scavenged across the moor by day and by night, sleeping only when they were completely exhausted.

It was the black Alsatian who dug out the first sheep. He had picked up her scent from the blow-hole which her breath made in the snow beneath which she was buried. He dug furiously until his strong forefeet partly uncovered the ewe which lay drugged by the cold and weakened by lack of food. The dogs, driven by hunger, tore at her haunches and throat, skilfully evading the feeble blows of her flailing hooves and the weight of her threshing body. That day they fed royally on rich red meat, and the body continued to feed them for another week. After that they starved again until the Alsatian dug out another ewe.

Spring came slowly. By the beginning of March snowfalls were rare and the strengthening sun was beginning to melt the icy drifts. Patches of rock began to stand out stark and black against the whiteness of the hillsides and here and there the brown stems of heather and bracken pierced the melting snow. Small streams which had flowed swiftly between deep banks became noisy torrents which rushed down the valleys bearing rocks, bushes and trees along with them. Suddenly the moor came alive. A buzzard stooped to his prey; rabbits scampered across the sopping turf and a group of ponies with foals at their heels wandered up from the lowlands. A sparrow, winter-thin, twittered from a rock pile . . .

It was lambing time. The sheep which had survived the winter in the open staggered weakly in search of nourishing grass. Many of them dropped dead lambs, and the dogs feasted on these. Sometimes the Alsatian pulled down a dying ewe so that the pack could gorge themselves on the meat.

The hill farmers taking stock of the damage done to their flocks by the blizzard found ewes and lambs which had been partly eaten, and on the few remaining patches of snow they saw the imprint of dogs' paws. Clearly there was truth in what they had suspected for a long time: there was a pack of feral dogs on the moor. A group of shepherds volunteered to take turns to lie in wait with a shotgun for the killers, and several times in the days which followed the pack was sighted, but always from a distance. The Alsatian quickly picked up the scent of the men and led the dogs aside. His skill in evading the men was remarkable, and many a story was told in the farmhouses about the intelligence of the 'big, black devil', but even more amazing to the farmers was the tale told by shepherd after shepherd about the little brown dachshund which scampered along in the wake of the pack, wheeling when they wheeled, part of the group yet separate from it, and always just out of gunshot.

It was his inability to keep up with the faster dogs which saved the small dog's life, for one day a lucky shot brought down the pack leader, and he rolled on the ground mortally wounded. The dogs which followed him were also hit, but the dachshund, far behind, stopped in his tracks and ran for cover as the shepherds followed the wounded animals shooting them down one by one. It was sunset, and the little dog managed to hide in a thicket of gorse bushes until nightfall, and then he slunk away across the moor.

The bitter winter was followed by a warm spring, and almost overnight the last greying patches of snow vanished. New grass and heather shoots sprang up, and the gorse bushes burst into golden flower. Snake-like fronds of bracken broke through the turf, and pale primroses and violets lined the banks of the snow-fed streams. Food was plentiful for the dog. Rabbits, heavy with young or nursing litters, nibbled the grass by their burrows, young birds flew clumsily from boulder to boulder, moles, voles, rats and other small animals sought food among the clitters after the long, hard winter months.

One evening as twilight fell, he disturbed a vixen with cubs playing on the hillside. At first he was puzzled by their strange smell – too pungent to be dog yet bearing some relationship to his kind. He lay and watched the cubs as they tumbled over each other and butted against their mother, but when the smallest cub, pushed by his playmates, rolled over and over down the hill towards him he darted out and would have seized it. The vixen, however was too quick for him. Baring her teeth and snarling ferociously she was upon him in one bound, and it was only by luck that he escaped with his life. One of the cubs, frightened by the sudden appearance of the dog, whimpered, and the mother fox was momentarily distracted by the sound so that the dachshund was able to roll from beneath her and run away. The vixen did not want to leave her cubs so she did not pursue him: after a moment or two she lay down and offered her teats to her young.

The dog fled into the bushes where he lay panting. As night fell he worked his way down the hillside, moving carefully and quietly for he did not want to attract the vixen's attention, but when he was well out of sight, hidden by rocks and a tall patch of cotton grass, he took to his heels and ran as fast as his short legs would carry him. Towards morning he slept in the lower reaches of a valley which ran like a deep cleft from the high moors to the lowlands. When the sun rose he stretched his aching limbs and trotted towards some cottages which clustered by a ford. It was many months since he had sought human company so he moved warily.

Chapter Six

The cottage which was nearest the dog was built on the banks of a stream. The garden behind it stretched upwards across the hillside. On its front steps, which raised it a little from a path alongside the water, a ginger cat lolled in the early morning sunshine. The dachshund eyed the cat suspiciously, but the animal appeared entirely unaware of his existence: it stretched one golden paw, twitched its tail and started to wash behind its ears. The dog advanced cautiously; the cat seemed unconcerned, although it stopped washing and cast a quick glance at the new arrival. The dachshund paused and sniffed the air: he could smell cooking, the mouth-watering odour of bacon sizzling in a hot pan. The smell seemed to come from the back of the house, but to go there he had to pass very close to the cat. He went forward slowly, not because he was afraid of the tom, but because he had lived in the wild for so long that he was wary of any strange animal.

When the cat leaped to its feet, arched its back and spat, he stopped. Then, recognizing the challenge, he ran forward barking, expecting the absurd creature to turn tail, but the cat had other ideas. A tough old animal, scarred by many battles, he knew no fear of dogs or any other creature. The cottage garden was his territory, and come what may he would protect it. As the dog advanced he launched himself, a streak of yellow fury, at the long brown body. His claws raked the dog's eyes and sank into the soft skin of his muzzle. The dachshund, amazed and half-blinded by the onslaught, turned to run away, but the cat leaped onto his back, sinking his claws into shoulder muscles, clinging tenaciously.

There was nothing that the dog could do. The cat clung to him as he ran away, its claws causing him agonizing pain. He tried to dislodge his attacker by scraping under the low branches of a rhododendron bush, but the tom flattened his body, sank his claws even deeper and hung on. The dachshund squealed with pain and rolled on the ground, flinging the cat aside, but the tom quickly returned to the attack, sinking teeth and claws into the dog's hind leg. The dachshund snapped at him and missed, and then as the cat rolled aside, scrambled to his feet and dashed off howling. The tom, unruffled, walked slowly back to the steps and started to wash again.

The dog ran the whole length of the cottages by the stream before he felt safe enough to slow down and take stock of his injuries. There was blood on his face, and his shoulders and hind leg were very sore. He waded into the brook to drink and found that the coldness of the water eased his pain. After a few moments he trotted along the path which led down the valley, shaking water from his forefeet and muzzle as he went. The sun was warm on his back and the ache in his muscles soon passed: he forgot the cat and thought only of food.

When the path ended he took to the fields, crossing pastures where cows grazed and skirting half-grown wheat. The ground was softer here than on the high moors and the air was warmer. Long forgotten scents tickled his nostrils – the smells of honeysuckle, clover and meadow flowers, ripening hay and rich, red soil. He found rabbit holes under a hazel hedge and chased a young rabbit into the open. The fresh meat satisfied his hunger: a crow shared the meal with him, stealing beakfuls of entrails and eating them while perched on the hazel boughs. When the dog left a squawking cloud of birds flew down to peck at the remains.

At sunset he was on the outskirts of a town. He sat by the side of a busy road and watched the lorries as they rumbled by. Petrol fumes, exhaust gases and dust made him sneeze, and the noise of the speeding vehicles made him frightened. He remembered the motorway where he had been abandoned and was filled with unease by the memory of long-past, unhappy things. The wounds that the cat had inflicted on his body still smarted, and he was hungry.

At last, he plucked up the courage to cross the road. There was a brief lull in the passing traffic so he sped across, his ears flapping, his eyes wild and his tail tucked well between his hind legs.

On the other side of the road was a wide grass verge and beyond it a low stone wall. The dog leaped over the wall and found himself in a park where an expanse of mown grass was broken by ornamental flower-beds and clumps of flowering trees. There was a strong smell of humans, and here and there were apple cores, paper bags, ice-cream cartons and half empty packets of crisps. He lifted a leg against a tree trunk, gobbled a few broken crisps, and trotted on his way.

The park-keeper, who was going on his evening round before locking the gates, first noticed the dachshund rooting in a flowerbed for a bone which another dog had hidden. The man told him to be off, then he noticed that the dog wore no collar. Rounding up strays was one of his duties so he pulled a collar and lead from his pocket and went after the animal.

It took him several minutes and a lot of persuasion to catch the dachshund, but eventually he had the little brown body securely held on the leash. The dachshund trembled when he patted him, but the man found a dog biscuit in the depths of his pocket and soon the dog was licking his hands in a friendly fashion. Together they went round the park, locking the gates and seeing that all was well for the night. Then the park-keeper led him home through the twilit streets of the town.

The roads were silent and deserted now that the day was over, but there were a few pedestrians on the pavements. The man noticed that the dog was nervous of people and he wondered as they crossed the town centre what unpleasant experience had made him so. 'There's no need to be afraid, my lad,' he said. 'You can stay with me tonight and then I'll take you to the dogs' home. If no-one claims you, maybe I'll keep you.'

The dachshund liked the little house where the man lived alone. He enjoyed the meal of biscuits and chopped meat which the man gave him, and he was grateful for the ointment which his new friend spread on his injuries. That night he slept on a pile of newspaper in a large cardboard carton, and he slept well and comfortably. The next day the man fed and petted him before putting him on his lead. They set off through the busy streets. The dachshund unused to the leash, pulled, and the man warned him sternly to behave himself. 'Right little tearaway, you are, my lad,' he said, but there was kindness in his voice.

The dogs' home was a large Victorian building on the far side of the town. Its garden, filled with concrete sheds and wooden lean-to shelters, housed tiers of kennels and was surrounded by a high wall. Long before they reached the place the dachshund could smell strange dogs and his quick ears detected the distant sound of their barking. He gave little excited yelps and tugged harder at his lead until the man yanked him back and flicked him with the end of the leather strap.

The yard in front of the house had been newly hosed and smelt of disinfectant, which made the dog wrinkle his nose and draw back his lips in distaste, but he was very excited by the knowledge

41

that there were other dogs close by. He could hardly stand still while the man filled in the form saying where he had been found, and he wriggled and twisted when a strange man picked him up and felt him all over with great care. At last he was pronounced healthy; his cat scratches which were already healing were passed over as minor injuries. They put him in a pen by himself, and gave him a bowl of drinking water and a handful of dog biscuits. The park-keeper petted him before he left. 'Do you think he'll be claimed?' he called to the attendant as he went out.

'Not likely. You can tell by his condition that he's been on the run for a long time. Maybe someone'll adopt him, else he's for the chop.'

'He's a nice little chap,' replied the park-keeper, 'and I could do with a small dog for company. I'll call in again in a day or two to see what's happened. If no-one else wants him, I'll have him.'

Chapter Seven

The first day in the dogs' home passed quickly because it was full of interest. People were coming and going all the time, and there were so many strange and interesting smells. Across the yard from the dachshund was a wire-haired terrier. It seemed that he had been in the place for several days because he was extremely bored. He dozed all day, lying with his head on his outstretched paws and his nose just under the wire netting which surrounded the bottom of the pen. He showed no sign of interest when anyone passed, but just occasionally the dachshund saw the gleam of his little black eyes under their half-closed lids, and knew that the animal was looking at him.

In the early evening, when the boy came round with his sack of biscuits, doling out the food to each enclosure, the terrier raised his head and gave a quiet 'woof.' The boy bent and scratched the dog's head and said, 'Cheer up, old man. There's still one more day. Perhaps someone will come for you tomorrow.' The terrier sighed. After the boy had gone he rose heavily to his feet and ate the biscuits slowly without much appetite. His despondency communicated itself to the dachshund who threw back his head and howled. Immediately the doleful sound was echoed by the other dogs all round the yard, and soon there was a pandemonium of wails, howls and barks. The warden, who was just about to go home for the night, came running to find out what was amiss, and when they saw him the dogs stopped howling and all barked hysterically. He went from pen to pen trying to quieten them, talking to each in turn, reaching through the bars to pat their heads, and holding out a hand for each to sniff. When he came to the dachshund he said, 'Twas you started them off, wasn't it boy? That won't do, you know. Mustn't wake the neighbours. Now settle down and sleep, there's a good chap. Tomorrow is another day.' The little dog licked his hand, and comforted, started to eat his biscuits.

That night he slept restlessly, not because he felt unsafe, but because there was something unpleasant about the atmosphere of the place — misery hung over it like a great black cloud. He whimpered a little to himself and when he slept his dreams were frightening.

The next day was worse. Late in the afternoon the wire-haired terrier was led away. He pulled at the lead and tried to sit, but the lad tugged so that his paws slid along the gound and he was forced to stand up and walk. The dachshund knew that something awful was going to happen, and again he howled and the other dogs howled with him. This time no-one came to quieten them.

There was meat for the evening meal, but even

the taste of good fresh horse did not lighten the dachshund's spirits. As soon as he had finished the food, he curled up and tried to sleep.

A new dog was put into the empty pen at midday. The newcomer was an Airedale, who obviously came from a good home. His eyes were bright, his coat well-groomed, and his sturdy body seemed to be in the pink of condition. A slight ruffling of the hair on his neck showed where a collar had rubbed. It looked as if he had broken loose from a tether and his collar had snapped and fallen off. He spent the afternoon pacing up and down in front of his sleeping-quarters, looking constantly towards the gate. Before the evening meal was brought round, a lady came to collect him. He leaped on her excitedly, trying to lick her face, but stood quietly enough while she buckled a collar round his neck and snapped a lead onto it. The dachshund saw them going towards the gate, the Airedale leaping and bounding exuberantly.

Slowly it was dawning on him that all the dogs in the home were lost. Some were reclaimed by their owners, but some were taken away to a dreadful fate. He knew in his bones that no-one would come for him. How could they? He was nobody's dog.

The next morning, when the boy brought his breakfast, he darted forward between the lad's legs, and made for the entrance. The boy ran after him shouting, and soon all the dogs were barking. He quickly realised that there was no easy way out through the gate: it was faced with wire netting and far too high to jump over. Dodging past the boy he circled the yard, trying to find a place where he might leap the walls, but the enclosure had been designed to be secure against far bigger dogs than he. There was no escape. The warden had joined the lad and they were advancing on him, arms spread, trying to drive him into a corner. For a moment he despaired, then, when all seemed lost, the gate opened and a butcher's van started to come through. The warden shouted, but the little dog had seized his chance. Darting between the warden's legs he sprinted through the opening and was away down the street. He heard shouts and pounding feet behind him, but regardless of the traffic he fled across roads, down side streets and through alleyways until all the sounds of pursuit had died away. At last, panting harshly, he found himself on a river bank. There was no-one in sight, so he gratefully crawled into a patch of nettles and slept the sleep of exhaustion.

The sun was already low in the sky when he awoke, and he felt cold and hungry. The river flowed by, smooth and brown, far too deep to swim across. Behind him lay the town, busy with people; he did not want to go in that direction – for that was the way to the dogs' home. The grass along the bank smelt of his kind: he trotted along sniffing at a bush here, a patch of reeds there. Under an alder tree he found a bone, but it was old and dry and there was no longer any nutriment in it. However, the discovery cheered him. It was while he was still investigating this that there was a strange noise, a hooting, and round the bend of the river came a boat. It passed quickly; the man at the wheel gave him scarcely a glance.

Still tired, he trotted slowly along the river path. A light rain was falling and his coat was beaded with moisture; his tongue lolled from the side of his mouth, but his head was filled with thoughts of juicy meat and crisp, crunchy biscuits. So real were his imaginings that he could smell the rich odours of stew; he licked his lips. It was not a dream, there really was stew somewhere. His lips were salty, but there was also a faint taste of cooked meat. His nostrils twitched and picked up the direction from which the scent came. He ran forward.

Where the river curved there were several barges moored against the bank, and from one of them there came the sound of pans and crockery being moved. A short plank led from the bank to the deck; without any hesitation the dachshund ran aboard. There was no-one to be seen, nor did there seem to be any way of following the fragrance of the food to its source somewhere below decks. He stood still and yapped, and listened, and yapped again. Presently a hatch opened and a tall, pale boy came out. He smiled when he saw the dog, and the dachshund flexed his front legs and jumped up and down. The lad held out his hand and the dog licked it, then turned his head to have his ears rubbed. 'Come on then, you rascal,' laughed the boy, 'let's get you some supper.' He went back into the boat and the dachshund followed him, a little doubtfully.

Below decks the bargee and his family were enjoying their meal. The woman gave the dog a dish of stew which he wolfed. When the plate was empty he turned it over and licked underneath to make sure that he had missed nothing. The woman laughed and brought another scoopful of meat and gravy for him: the boy sat on the floor and watched. 'I *can* keep him, Dad, can't I?' he pleaded. 'He's lost, he's nobody's dog.'

'You ought to take him to the police station,' the man replied. 'He looks neglected, but he may belong to somebody.'

'Oh, Dad!'

When the woman was washing the dishes and the man had gone on deck, the lad put the dog on a leash of string and took him ashore, calling out to his father as they went, but about twenty minutes later he crept back to the boat with the dachshund hidden under his jacket. His father was busy with the engine, his mother had her back turned, so he smuggled the dog below decks and hid him in the blankets on his bunk. The dachshund was warm and full of food so he slept. The lad called 'Good-night' to his parents and climbed into bed. Dog and boy slept covered by the same blankets.

Soon after dawn broke the barge moved away from its mooring and set off downstream. The gentle chugging of its engine woke the dachshund who crawled from his hiding-place and licked the boy's face. The lad put out a sleepy hand and caressed the sleek head: then cuddled close together, they both slept again.

When the woman came to waken her son she was amazed to see the dog sleeping on the bunk. She told her husband that the dog was still aboard and begged him not to be angry with their son. 'It's the first time he's shown any interest in anything since his illness,' she said. 'The dog's just a stray. Let's keep him.'

'Well, it *is* a long way back,' the man grumbled, 'but I'm sure we're doing wrong. Still, have it your way. If the lad's happy . . .' At the same time, back at the dogs' home, the park-keeper was enquiring about the dachshund and was upset to hear that he had run off, 'I told you I'd have him,' he complained. 'I thought he was safe enough here.'

'We thought he was safe, too,' answered the warden, 'but the little rascal was as quick as a cat and as slippery as an eel. He was away before you could say "Jack Robinson", but he'll turn up again. He belongs to nobody.'

The park-keeper went sadly away.

Chapter Eight

The barge moved slowly downstream. The town was left far behind and they were passing through rich, farming country. On either bank cows grazed in the lush green water meadows, and on the gentle hill-slopes golden fields of ripening grain rippled silently in the summer breeze. Scarlet poppies and tall, purple foxgloves grew close by the water's edge; kingfishers skimmed along the canal taking their insect prey, and the bright world was over-hung by a huge blue sky.

The boy and the dog romped on deck, and when their play became too boisterous the bargee put them ashore to run and roll together on the tow-path. They played throw-and-fetch, and catch-me-if-you-can, laughing and yelping and falling over each other in the sunshine. Sometimes they raced ahead of the barge and hid in the bushes only to jump out with wild shouts and raucous barks as the craft drew level with them. At other times they allowed the boat to snake out of sight around a series of bends, and then they cut across country to draw ahead of it, so that they could appear sitting quietly on the bank just as the boy's mother was worriedly peering astern.

During the next fortnight the barge went up and down canals and rivers fetching and carrying various cargoes. Colour came into the boy's cheeks and his eyes grew bright and merry. The dog too, looked well: his coat, which his new master groomed every evening, grew smooth and glossy, his eyes sparkled, and his muscular little body rippled under a thin layer of fat. He ate hugely and he exercised to the point of exhaustion, sleeping each night cosily curled against his master. He was sure that at last he had found a human who would never desert him.

Once, when the barge was waiting at a lock for the gates to open, the dachshund leaped for the boat onto the slippery barrier. His claws skidded madly on the weed-covered wood, and for a moment it looked as if he would fall to be washed away in the water which was foaming downstream. The bargee shouted, the lock-keeper ran out; the boy called desperately. After one heart-stopping minute the dog regained his balance and trotted confidently across the opening gate. The lock-keeper ran to his wheel, but the barge had already sunk several feet below the top of the barrier. It seemed that the little dog was marooned and would have to make a perilous return trip towards the lock-keeper's cottage. Then suddenly, as if he realised what was happening, the dachshund took a flying leap which landed him on the roof of the barge's wheel-house, from which his young master rescued him.

'Don't ever do anything like that again, Dachsie,' scolded the lad as he hugged the animal to him and fondled his ears. The lock-keeper was shaking his head, and the bargee was scowling, but the boy and his dog were wrapped up in each other.

The long summer days passed slowly. Always there was something new for the boy and the dachshund to do. Sometimes, after the barge had moored for the night, they roamed the fields coming back with the lad's jacket pockets stuffed with tiny pink-gilled mushrooms, sometimes they chased rabbits along the hedgerows and often the dog brought one back in his jaws. But once, when the woman sent them over the meadows to fetch milk, butter and eggs from a farm, the boy wondered to see that the dog walked dispiritedly with a drooping tail as they crossed the farmyard. He could not know that his friend was remembering another farmyard where the farmer was loud-voiced and unfriendly and there was a man with a gun . . .

That night the dog slept uneasily. In the distance a calf bawled at the moon and a cow lowed. The sounds and the smells of the farmyard were strong in his nostrils, and they reminded him of an old, half-forgotten sadness. He twitched and whimpered in his sleep.

A little more than two weeks after leaving the town, the canal in which they were travelling widened and joined a broad, smooth flowing river. The bargee cut the engine and for much of the time the craft floated noiselessly downstream. When the river became crowded with other vessels, he was forced to use power again and once more the boat vibrated to the familiar chug-chug from the engine housing. No longer could the boy and the dog play on the river banks, so they spent much of their time lying together on the deck in the sunshine watching the assorted craft which moved this way and that on the broad surface of the stream. One afternoon a large bird with a powerful, curved, yellow beak and silver-grey wings alighted on the wheel-house. The dachshund, who had never seen its like before, watched it interestedly and manoeuvred nearer to it. The bird strutted up and down, one keen eye noting the dog's stealthy movements. At last frustrated by the fact that he was unable to climb onto the wheel-house, the dachshund stood on his hind legs and yapped wildly, at which the bird gave a derisive cackle and flew off. Soon the sky was filled by a crowd of similar birds which flew over the water, trailing their legs and crying. Towards sunset they came together in a cloud which wheeled and flew away into the distance.

'Seagulls are roosting early, tonight, son,' said the man. 'Could be a sign of bad weather.'

As darkness fell they came into a busy estuary. The banks were crowded with houses, and there was a noise of machinery and a distant hum of traffic. The dog smelled the familiar town smells which reminded him of the dogs' home, and he whined mournfully. When a train rumbled along a track he shivered against his master's leg, and he lost his zest for play. The smells of motor oil, petrol, fumes and dust were very unpleasant to him. He cowered behind a pile of coiled rope until he was coaxed, quivering, to stand by his master in the stern of the vessel and watch the litter-strewn water which rippled out in their wake.

They tied up to a quay for the night. Alongside the barge were other gaily-painted narrow boats with families aboard. Everyone seemed to know everyone else and there was a happy air of reunion. The boy leaped from boat to boat chattering to this one and that one. The dog sniffed at the new smells and explored the quay. Gradually he relaxed and accepted scraps of food from men working on the wharves, but always his eyes roved back to where his master talked with his friends. They slept moored to the quayside, the boat rising and falling on a faint sea swell. At dawn they were awakened by the gulls which quarrelled and shrieked on the harbourside. The weather had worsened: a small, incessant rain was falling.

On the second day the boy clambered ashore and made towards the harbour gates, the dachshund close at his heels. The stone-cobbled quay shone wetly and a black ooze made the going slippery. Boy and dog walked slowly, despondently.

The town was crowded with people and with traffic. Trucks lined the road from the dock waiting their turn to move in to load or unload. A railway line ran from the quayside into the town.

The boy and dog mooched from street to street, stopping to stare in shop windows, pausing at pedestrian crossings, halting at kerb stones. Both were cold and wet and the dachshund's underparts were stiff with black mud. When other dogs approached him he growled irritably.

At mid-day they made their way back to the quays where the boy stopped at a kiosk to buy chocolate. The dog pottered between the warehouses out of the wind, and stalked a seagull which flew away as soon as he drew near it. The bird fluttered for several yards and then alighted again, its wicked yellow eyes daring the animal to follow it. Exasperatedly the dachshund rushed after it, all his boredom and unhappiness expressing itself in his determination to catch the arrogant bird, but the gull evaded him, flying along the wharf in short bursts. The dog heard his master's call, but for once he ignored it. His need to catch the tantalising bird had become obsessive, and he was soon lost to the boy's sight.

At last the gull alighted on a heap of grain in a chute above a railway truck. It was only a few feet above the dog's head, and a flight of stairs led up to it. The dachshund scrambled up and pounced onto the corn, but the bird had flown. At the same moment the chute opened, and grain and dog fell into the truck below. At first the animal lay dazed and shaken, afraid to move. The corn shifted beneath him like sand, and the dust made him sneeze. Then, almost before he had time to collect himself, the chute opened again and a fresh load of grain was deposited on him so that he was completely buried.

Chapter Nine

He lay half-stunned, but as the shock passed he struggled frantically to free himself from the corn which covered him. It was like trying to scramble out of a bog: there was no firm foothold anywhere. The stuff went up his nose, into his mouth, eyes and ears so that he thought that he would suffocate, yet the more he struggled the deeper he sank into the soft mound. His movements grew weaker and weaker until one flailing foot struck something hard — one of the strengthening ribs which ran along the side of the truck. He floundered towards it until both front paws were securely hooked over the wooden support, and slowly he levered up his body until his muzzle broke through the surface of the grain, and he was able to gulp in deep breaths of fresh air. The strain on his fore-paws was terrific since he was still unable to gain a firm purchase with his hind legs, but he managed to hang on while his head cleared. Then, slowly exerting all the power in his tough little body, he moved paw after paw along the rib until he reached the rear end of the vehicle. He could see very little for the truck had been sheeted over with tarpaulin, but some little light filtered in beneath the edges of the covering. In this faint glow he saw that in one corner the tarpaulin was folded so that part of it lay across the surface of the grain. Somehow he worked his way to this small island, which held firm although it sank a little under his weight. Exhausted he lay there panting and after a while he slept.

He was awakened sharply by a rumbling and a grinding followed by a severe jolting which almost threw him from his resting place. The truck was in motion and rapidly gaining speed. He whimpered with terror and crouched on his piece of tarpaulin. As the vehicle sped forwards the motion and the noise became even more terrifying. The grain container was one in a long series of goods trucks which were bumping and swaying along the track. It was a long while before the dog gained enough courage to peer through the chinks between the tarpaulin and the edge of the vehicle. At first he was unable to focus on the flying countryside, but his nostrils twitched as the salt tang of the sea gave way to the scent of fields. The blur of green, broken only by the dark finger of a tree or the brick-red stain of a cluster of houses, meant nothing to him, but as he gradually grew accustomed to the speed and motion of the train he found that he could distinguish cows grazing in the meadows, sheep staring vacantly into space and horses galloping, tails flying in the wind. The slow-moving hills formed an ever-changing backdrop to the fields of golden wheat and the pastures which sped rapidly past alongside the track. Once a farm dog ran barking down a lane towards the railway line and the dachshund barked back, his hackles rising at what he took to be a personal challenge, but almost at once the dog was whisked from his sight and he was left standing indignantly on his patch of tarpaulin.

The noise of the train grew louder and harsher as the engine shot into a tunnel. The sudden darkness shocked the dog who crouched again upon his stomach and shivered with fear. When the noise lessened and daylight filtered through between the truck and its covering once more, he thrust his nose through the opening and howled.

The train rushed on endlessly. Fields gave way to towns, towns to moors, villages, farmsteads and other fields. The day passed slowly, but the dog was too frightened to feel hunger or to sleep for more than a few moments at a time.

At nightfall the engine braked sharply, each truck catapulting into the next. The dachshund was unable to keep his balance and lay on his side afraid to move as the train jogged over a series of points and came to a halt in a goods-yard. After the final jolt the motion ceased and everything was still and quiet. Cautiously the dog climbed up to peer through his peep-hole. It was almost completely dark outside, but he could just make out the shapes of trucks around him and the long grey line of a road which snaked away into the darkness. The air smelled stale, rank with engine oil and diesel fumes.

When he was sure that all movement had

ceased, his confidence returned, and he tried to force his way under the tarpaulin, but the ropes which held the covering were too tightly tied. He worried at the knots, fraying and loosening them with his teeth, but it was almost dawn before the last strands snapped and he could escape. The jump from the top of the truck onto the trackway jarred his back: he felt stiff and cold and very, very miserable. As he picked his way across the cold iron rails, he lifted his muzzle and tested the air. Although he could identify many of the scents none of them was friendly, none bore any hint of the place where he had left his young master. He knew that the town where the seagulls roamed the quays was very far away, and he was filled with a great sadness.

It was somewhile before he found the exit from the goods-yard. The sun was already risen into a milky sky when he came to a place where a long, grey street, flanked by tall houses, stretched into the distance. He paused to scratch some of the engine oil from his pads and to relieve himself against a plane tree with white-patched bark. There was nowhere to go except straight on. He was tired, frightened and depressed, but with indomitable courage he ran on.

Chapter Ten

The long street led to a tree-lined square surrounded by tall houses. Already the human world was astir: a milkman clattered his crates, a postman slapped mail into letterboxes and sleepy-eyed people came from the houses to drive off in cars or to hurry along the pavements. The place smelt like a town, and all the scents were unpleasant. A tabby cat scratched and yawned at the top of a flight of steps, pausing to arch her back and hiss at the dog as he passed. He scurried on with drooping tail and ears flattened. In an overturned waste bin at the end of the square he found a half-eaten ham sandwich which he swallowed in one gulp; in the gutter he found part of a pork pie. The meat was stale and rancid, but he was far too hungry to be choosy. He ran on, crossing street after street, square after square. It was now broad daylight and the roads were busy with traffic. On the pavements the dog dodged between hurrying feet, occasionally accidentally entangling with a pair of trousered legs: once, a well-aimed kick caught him on his flank. He ran on, filled with the one thought, that he must get out of this strange place and find the barge and his young master again. The town seemed endless.

At mid-day he followed the scent of food to a yard at the back of a restaurant. From beneath a closed door the smell of meat and vegetables crept out. There were people there too because he could hear voices and the clatter of crockery. Even the rubbish bins which stood against the wall smelt of meat. He stood on his hind legs and tried to pull one over, but he was too small and had not the necessary body weight. He did, however, succeed in knocking the lid off, and it fell noisily to the ground. The door opened and a man came out.

'What the dickens are you doing, Browny?' he asked, 'I've not see you round here before. It's hungry you are, is it?' He went into the restaurant and came out with a plate laden with scraps, muttering to himself, 'A sucker for stray dogs I am. More fool me.'

The dachshund fell on the food and ate greedily. The man bent to pat him, but he was far too busy to notice. When the man returned into the building and the door clicked shut, he raised his head for a moment, but otherwise the food held all his attention.

After his meal he looked round for a place where he could sleep. Across the road was a park bounded by iron railings. The lawns were uncut and the shrubberies overgrown; obviously humans did not bother with it very much. It was quiet and it smelt of grass and flowers. He burrowed deep into a patch of bushes and slept, but his sleep was broken by dreams for he whimpered quietly and his legs moved as if he were running.

He woke when the western sky was losing colour and darkness was crowding in from the east. The park was deserted. The dachshund rose and stretched and lifted his nose to the breeze. A scent of honeysuckle hung on the air.

He crossed the road to the restaurant, but the door was firmly closed and the waste bins had been emptied. He scratched at the doorstep and barked, but the sound was swallowed in the clatter of dishes and the noise of a record player. Presently, he wandered off disconsolately.

That night he slept in the park. He was cold and hungry and sleep came slowly. In the morning he was wakened by the sound of church bells. The streets were quiet and almost free from traffic. The restaurant too, was bathed in silence; there was no smell of warm food. He hung about the yard for a long while, but no-one came. Tired and stiff he lay down on the pavement in the sunshine and dozed: soon he would be on his way again.

He became alert at the sound of claws tapping on the paving stones near him and at the strong scent of dog. A cairn terrier was flexing her fore-paws and inviting him to play. He eyed her warily. She was an old dog and her coat was tattered and unkempt, but her eyes were bright and her pink tongue lolling from the side of her mouth was clean and healthy. When he did not move she lay on her stomach a few feet from him and grinned, her skimpy tail thumping the ground. The dachshund inched towards her, his tail swishing: he needed a friend, if friend she was. They touched noses and smelled each other, and the bitch rolled over to show her stomach. They chased each other up and down the street, and when the terrier lay down panting and exhausted, the dachshund extended his muzzle towards her so that she could lick his nose and eyes. He sensed that she, too, was friend-less and without a home.

When the terrier had rested, they crossed the road into the park and played around the flower-beds, but suddenly the bitch turned and ran pur-posefully across the street, looking over her shoulder at the dog and inviting him to follow. She went straight to the back of the restaurant and barked loudly, scrabbling at the step. There was a sound of movement within. In a few moments the man came out with a plate of food. When he saw the dachshund he laughed. 'Got yourself a mate, have you, Daisy? I've seen him before, too. Well, there's plenty of scraps — neither of you need go hungry.' He went back into the kitchen and brought out some ox-liver and a ham bone which the two dogs worried between them. When they were stuffed with food the terrier led the way to the park.

The dachshund was happier than he had been since he had left his young master. For the time being he was content to settle down with his new friend, sleeping curled against her in a sheltered spot among the bushes, eating at the restaurant and exploring the town. Days turned into weeks, summer burned into autumn. The bitch seemed less playful and friendly than she had been. When the dog nudged her ribs she snapped at him. Often she lay for hours in the long grass and would not move. One sunny morning she ran through the park exploring it as though it were strange territory. Eventually she thrust her way behind some bushes where the park was bounded by a length of ruined wall. At the foot of the masonry was a cavity filled with dried leaves and completely hidden from the main body of the pleasure ground by a screen of cotoneasters. The dog tried to follow his mate into the hole, but she snapped at him so he stood at a distance and watched her as she trampled the leaves and made herself a nest. She would not come out for food so he ate alone. When he came back from his meal he was amazed to hear a strange whimpering sound from her hiding-place. He approached very cautiously, only to find that the terrier was suckling three tiny puppies. She looked at him proudly, but dared him to come any closer. That night he slept beneath the cotoneasters, but he wakened frequently to creep through the grasses to look at his family. Each time the bitch saw him she gave a low growl which warned him not to come too close.

In a day or two she was up and about again, demanding food from the restaurant. Her appetite was insatiable, and she drank deeply of the milk which the man now provided as an extra. After her meal she returned to the nest to clean and care for her youngsters.

They grew quickly. Two of them looked like rough coated dachshunds with terrier heads. One looked like a tiny cairn terrier, with a dachshund's long smooth tail.

The bitch, thanks to the kindness and understanding of the restaurant owner, was able to feed her pups well so that they grew strong and healthy. As they grew older she allowed her mate to come into the nest and even to lick the puppies' heads, but at night she drove him away to sleep on his own.

By the time the first leaves were falling from the trees in the park the youngsters had grown thick, furry coats and were able to tumble through the grasses outside the nest. They gave their mother no peace. One after another they crawled over her back where she lay resting, nipped her ears and chewed her tail until even *her* patience was exhausted and she cuffed them or held them down with her paw. They no longer obeyed her implicitly, and she often found it difficult to keep them from straying onto the paths outside the shrubbery. She scurried to the restaurant for her food and scurried back to round up the pups from wherever they had wandered. One morning, unnoticed by her, a pup stumbled after her onto the roadway. Suddenly there was a squeal of brakes and the tiny body flew high in the air. The bitch, returning from her food, sniffed at the bloodied corpse, carried it a few steps, and then put it down, realizing that her puppy was dead. She hurried off to her living family, anxious lest they, too, might have come to some harm. The needs of her two surviving young quickly drove all thoughts of the dead pup from her mind: only at night she felt a cold place where the third little body should have lain tucked against her side, and sometimes she whimpered in her sleep.

Chapter Eleven

It was a mild autumn, but the terrier knew that she needed to find a warmer, drier home for her family before the winter set in. As soon as they were weaned, she led the puppies by night to some waste ground on the outskirts of the town. The place had been used as a rubbish dump. Old cars surrounded by derelict prams, bicycle frames, torn mattresses and other household refuse littered the ground. It was an ideal home for the dogs. At first the bitch settled in the half-open boot of a car, but the rain came in and it was draughty. Later she found a section of sewage pipe which lay with one end buried in a mound of ash and rubble, the other hidden in a tangle of brambles and ivy. The cautious mother took a long time to satisfy herself that the pipe was the right home for family. She smelled the surround carefully and decided that it was a long while since human feet had walked there. She investigated the inside of the pipe and found it half full of leaves and dried grass. At the far end was a heap of mouldering sacks, dragged there by some boys to make a hideaway, but the hessian was full of mouse droppings and a spider's web stretched thickly from wall to wall, so she was sure that the place had not been used recently. It was just the sort of home that she was looking for, and she called the puppies in, nudging them onto the sacks. The dachshund who had followed the family trek from the park to the waste ground, would have settled down with his mate and the two youngsters, but she drove him away, snarling angrily. It was plain that short visits on his part were acceptable, but that until the pups were older she wanted him to keep his distance. He understood her anxieties and curled up near the mouth of the pipe where he could watch his family and guard against any danger which threatened them.

The pups liked their new home; there were so many exciting smells. Everything was new and strange. When the rain fell the noise of it beating on the pipe kept them jumping up and down with excitement. When the wind howled outside they stalked imaginary enemies towards the mouth of their dwelling only to run back to their mother when the noise became too loud. On sunny days they played outside, chasing dead leaves, or pretending to dig for bones. Their games were watched by both their mother and the dachshund. They grew wiry and strong.

There was little food for the dogs on the waste ground, but the adult animals returned daily to the restaurant where they ate their fill. The bitch carried home bones and pieces of meat which the youngsters enjoyed so that they never went hungry for long. She also caught mice and taught her babies to snap them by the necks so that they died instantly. Soon the puppies were climbing all over the rubbish tip from smell to exciting smell. Their only fear was of the huge brown rats which sat combing their whiskers in the pale sunshine. They watched their mother snap a rat to death, but the creatures were far too big and fierce for the puppies themselves to tackle.

The winter passed quickly. By Christmas the young dogs were following their mother to the restaurant where the man fed them too. By early spring they were running off on their own into the town and spending longer and longer periods away from the pipe. The bitch allowed the dachshund to sleep curled up with her inside the nest, and sometimes all four dogs snuggled up together.

The dog had weathered the winter well. He was sleek and muscular and his coat shone from the lickings which the bitch gave it. The terrier, on the other hand, looked unkempt and scrawny. She was several years older than her mate and had lived rough for longer than she could remember. Repeated litters of puppies had worn her out, and often she was very tired and breathless. On bright days, when the sun shone over the tip making the old cans shine like silver and bringing an amber glow to the empty beer bottles, the bitch lay outside the pipe, her flanks heaving gently. Sometimes the pain in her chest was very bad. One day in early spring she crawled into a clump of nettles where she lay panting. One of the young dogs crept in beside her and tried to tease her into play, but she licked his head and turned away. Once or twice she lifted her nose to the breeze. Soon she slept: she did not wake again.

The young dogs quickly accepted their mother's death. For a few more weeks they slept in the pipe, but the dachshund was peevish and short-tempered. One day they left the waste ground and did not return.

The dachshund stayed on, sleeping in the nest at night and going to the restaurant for food, but he felt restless. Bluebells were springing up between the rubbish where the earth was deep enough to nourish them, and their scent reminded the dog of the fields around the farm. He roamed further and further from the pipe each day, exploring the woods and pastures south of the town. Then one lovely morning he climbed the ridge that till now had formed his horizon. A vast patchwork of fields rolled away before him to where, in the distance, a faint grey-blue line lay stretched like a serpent between earth and sky. The gentle southerly breeze brought to him a scent that he remembered only too well – the salt tang of the sea. He lifted his nose and sniffed and thought of the quays where the grey-winged seagulls strutted and called, the warm comfort of the barge rocking on the long sea swell, the loving kindness of his young friend – the only master whom he completely trusted. He did not return to the town that day but set off towards the sea.

Chapter Twelve

The countryside through which he passed was mainly farmland. Fields of corn rippled silently in the wind. Young rabbits were plentiful in the hedgerows so that he did not go short of food. At night he slept in whatever shelter he could find, sometimes an empty barn, sometimes among the bushes in a copse, sometimes in a patch of nettles which he trod flat. Daily the smell of the sea grew stronger, but it was a long, long way to the coast. It was almost a week before he crossed the last field, forded a sluggish stream and came to a marsh which was bounded on its far side by sand dunes. He stopped at the stream to quench his thirst. The spring sun rose high in the sky, and he was very warm. He sat in a tuft of rushes and listened – the sounds were wrong. Instead of the bustle of the quays, the throb of engines, the clatter of cranes, he heard the whisper of the wind through the grasses and the lonely piping of a curlew along the shore. But the smell of the sea drew him on: he climbed the dunes, pushing through the marram grass, shouldering aside spikey sea poppies and the coarse stems of sea lavender. The sand beneath his paws was constantly shifting so that it reminded him of the grain in the goods truck. Often he slipped back further than he advanced, but he gamely struggled on. At last, hot and panting, he reached the crest of the sand hills and there before him lay the blue stretch of the sea. A gentle sandy slope, littered with mussel shells and slipper limpets ran down to the edge of the water. He picked his way across it, pausing to sniff at a pungent bunch of bladder wrack, a tangle of whelk eggs, a piece of driftwood. The sea was pleasantly cool around his ankles: he lapped a little but found that it was not good to drink. At a loss what to do next, he stood watching the waves creaming along the shore. A gull flapped lazily overhead, but there were no humans anywhere. Suddenly, he felt very much alone.

He spent the day scouring the beach for food, and in the evening he returned to the dunes where he found a small tidal creek, its banks lined with the fleshy stalks of samphire, its sand pimpled with worm casts. He was hungry for he had only eaten a sea-soaked bun and a piece of rotten fish. A water rat drinking unwarily from the brackish stream provided him with his evening meal, and feeling more satisfied, he dug a hollow in the warm sand beneath a wild lupin bush, and there he slept.

He awoke to a mother-of-pearl morning. The sun shining through a sea mist bathed everything in a rose-tinted, ever-changing light. Shapes and outlines were blurred and dim, and the dog found it difficult to know where he was. He made his way towards the only sound that he could recognize –

the slow gasp of the sea. When he reached the water's edge the mist lifted and he found that he stood on a gleaming tide-washed beach. The light reflected from the sea was dazzling: it hit him like a blow so that he ran, ears flopping, along the edge of the water. Dunling and curlew rose at his approach, but he kept straight on, heading for the dark shape of the headland which he could see in the distance. His wild gallop set the blood pounding in his veins and gave him a feeling of exhilaration.

The rocks at the base of the headland were cold, wet and slippery with seaweed, but he scrambled over them. Soon he had rounded the point, and there before him was a beach with boats and huts and all the signs of human habitation. He yammered with joy and ran on. In no time at all he was scampering up some steps which led to a promenade running along the top of the sea wall. Before him was a harbour where men were working and fishing-boats were tied up. He rushed up to them excitedly, tail swishing, barking with excitement and dancing with delight, but not one of the men took any notice. Only a black and white mongrel which was lying beside a man who was mending a net, sprang to his feet, his hackles up and growling fiercely. The dachshund saw trouble ahead and stood, his eyes blazing, lips curled back and legs stiff. He was not seeking a fight, but he was not the dog to allow himself to be bullied. The mongrel ran in, snapping at his throat, missing and tearing an ear. The dachshund closed his jaws on the other dog's foreleg and ripped away a chunk of hair and flesh. Both dogs were snarling and barking in fury, locked in fierce combat. Then there was a noise of human voices, and the dachshund felt a hand gripping his tail, but he tightened his grip on his opponent's flesh. A bucketful of icy water fell on him, and gasping and growling he was torn free from the other dog and held by the scruff of his neck. The mongrel, with a bloodied nose and torn leg, was being held by the man who had been mending the net.

'We'll have no more of that,' cried an authoritative voice. 'Put Skip in the boat shed for a while, Tom.'

'Doan' see why I should. Why should Skip suffer? He's more right here than that 'un. Chase 'un back where 'ee came from.'

There was a loud confused argument, then Skip was bundled away. Someone made a rough collar and lead from a piece of rope and slipped it over the dachshund's head. A man dragged him away.

'Doan' rightly know who you be, old chap, nor where you comes from,' said the man who held the lead. The dachshund sniffed at his boots which reeked of fish and trotted along beside him. 'I'll just call in at the police station and tell them I've got you in case anyone enquires. Then I'll take you home along of me. You'm a right saucy little dog with plenty of sperret an all, I warrant, an' I could do with a bit of company.'

The man lived in a house quite near the beach. He seemed to live alone because there were no smells of other humans in the place. The strong scent of his tobacco was in every room – the windows were tight shut – but the dog quickly decided that this could be the smell of home. He would accept this man as master even if he could not love him as he had learned to love the lad on the barge.

The man fed him and gave him water to drink, then he cleaned his wounds and put soothing ointment on them. That night the dachshund slept on the mat outside the man's bedroom door.

Chapter Thirteen

The dog quickly settled down in his new home. His torn ear and the long gash in his shoulder healed well, and soon he was perfectly fit again. Time passed, and no-one enquired at the police station about a lost dachshund, so the man was able to keep him. His new master reminded the dog a little of the farmhand whose cottage had been his first real home, a little of the park-keeper who had housed him overnight, and a little of the lad on the barge. He shared with them the same capacity for kindness and the same concern for the dog's well-being. The animal accepted him as his friend, but he no longer felt that he could completely trust any human being, except the bargee's son; he had been let down too often.

At first the fisherman, for such he was, left the dog shut in the house when he went to work. He came home later tired and wet and smelling of fish. There was always a plump cod fillet, a piece of dogfish or even a lump of shark's flesh for the dachshund's next meal. The man kept irregular hours, for his work was dependent on the time of the tides, but the dog always knew his step coming down the street, and was always waiting by the door to greet him on his entry. The fisherman patted him and tugged gently at his ears, the dog responded, swishing his tail from side to side and jumping up and down. The friendship between them grew.

The man found a collar and lead and took the dachshund for long walks along the sands and over the cliff tops. As soon as they were out of the village, the lead was removed so that the animal could run free. He fetched sticks which his master threw and rushed along the sea's edge barking at gulls, but most of all he loved to run on the beach when the moon was tipping the waves with silver and the waterline was a faint phosphorescence on the sand. In the pale light the rocks became monsters, enemies lurked in every patch of shadowed weed and the world was full of smells to be cautiously investigated. He loved to frighten himself with imaginary dangers, which he knew in his heart of hearts did not exist. Always there was the comforting plod of his master's boots along the shore behind him, and when his imagination overcame his good sense, he ran back for reassurance.

Spring passed into summer. The days were long, sunlit and calm. A sparkling sea crawled endlessly along the shore. The rock pools at the foot of the headland glowed red with sea anemones: small fish darted between the weeds, and tiny, green crabs scuttled over the patches of sand. The dog waded and swam to his heart's content, the fisherman watched him fondly. Almost against his will the dachshund found that he was beginning to trust and love the man. One morning the man called the dog to him. 'Jerry, lad, you're going to come out in the boat with me today. I'm going to make a sea-dog out of you.' When he left the house the dog followed him, barking excitedly and dancing along the street.

On board the boat the fisherman shut the animal in the cabin at first, but when they were well away from the land and he had time to spare he attached a long cord to the dachshund's collar and tied him to the wheel house. He thought that the dog had certainly been on a boat before – he showed no fear, although his sea legs were a little shakey. After an hour or so, when he saw that the animal was moving confidently, he removed the cord and let the dachshund run free.

They fished by day and by night throughout that summer. Sometimes the man sailed alone with the dog, taking mackerel, whiting or pollack on his troll lines. Sometimes they sailed with a group of seamen on a larger boat and put out a trawl net which brought in scoops of squirming fish. On these occasions the dog prudently kept out of the way, but he was a great favourite with all the fishermen. He loved their company, and he loved to be on the boat when the nets came in, but most of all he loved to be heading for home in a stiff breeze with the waves singing past the gunwhales and the engine throbbing steadily. He would stand in the bows, head held high, gazing intently shore-wards, ready to bark at the first glimpse of land. Sometimes the fisherman stood beside him, and the dog would ape his stance, raising one forepaw onto an upturned crate, exactly as the man stood. This brought roars of laughter from the other men, and the dog laughed with them and continued to clown.

The mongrel with whom he had fought on the day on which he first came to the village belonged to a younger fisherman, a friend of his master. The two dogs met frequently, and after an initial period when they regarded each other with suspicion, walking stiff-legged with hackles raised, tense with excitement, they gradually relaxed and became friends. Often they went on fishing trips together, and the men were amused to see the strangely assorted pair posed in the bows of the boat or sleeping curled nose to tail on a pile of rope.

The mongrel pretended a great contempt for seagulls. Often the birds swooped down when the nets were coming in, to seize fish and to swallow them whole. Quite large mackerel and medium sized flatfish went down their throats in one gulp, and their necks bulged sideways as they swallowed. The fishermen swore at them and tried to frighten them away, while the dachshund ran at them in little short rushes, but the mongrel ignored them completely. On one occasion, however, when the trawl had spilled an extra large catch into the body of the boat, the mongrel was nipped on the nose by the pincers of a huge crab at which he was sniffing. He yelped loudly and shook his head to free himself. The crab fell on the deck where a gull immediately pecked at it. For some reason the dog blamed the bird for his pain and snapped at it. At once the sky was filled with a squalling, milling crowd of gulls which swooped and dived at the boat and especially at the dogs. The dachshund stood amidships and barked at them, but the mongrel fled to the safety of the hatchway. The fishermen beat at the birds with empty fish creels, and for several minutes the air was loud with screaming birds and cursing men. Then someone emptied a skip of fish guts over the stern and at once the gulls fell back to gorge on the delicacies.

The boat sailed on. The dachshund quietened, and the mongrel came out of his hiding-place. They stood together in the bows while the fishing continued.

When the day was over they sailed into port with an empty basket at the mast head to signify a full catch, and a cloud of circling gulls followed astern.

Chapter Fourteen

The golden summer passed slowly, but gradually the mornings grew darker and colder and the evenings grew longer. On the cliffs the tamarisk lay in tumbled swathes. The gardens of the cottages by the hill were full of the tart, autumnal smell of apples. Dulse and wrack were washed up along the beach, and the sea grew wild and grey, shadowed by a lowering sky. In the early mornings the dog smelled the nose-tingling smell of frost and on the boat he spent much of his time in the engine house. As the seas grew rougher he learned to steady himself against the pitch and toss of the boat by standing with his paws well apart and his legs braced.

'A real sea-dog I've made of 'un,' laughed his master pulling the animal's ears affectionately.

The boats continued to fish throughout October although the weather was poor and their catches small, but towards the end of the month the smaller less seaworthy vessels tied up in harbour where they would remain all the winter. The crews joined together to work a few large boats and to share the profits. The dachshund's master and the owner of Skip, the mongrel, continued to work in one of the smaller craft. Two or three times a week they ventured out on the choppy seas to where they had set lobster pots on a rocky bottom; but the weather was wrong. Often they lost catches because they could not hold the boat steady in the rough water. They planned to beach their boat early in November since they had not the gear nor the craft to face the winter storms. The younger man intended to join with one of the larger vessels: the older fisherman was going to spend the dark months ashore.

On the day before their last scheduled trip the sun rose red in a sky of gun-metal grey. The horizon was blurred with mist and heavy clouds were building up in the west. Along the sea shore the ceaseless grind of pebbles flung backwards and forwards by the breakers could be heard as a thunderous roar under the crash of the waves. The dachshund's master scanned the horizon: 'Reckon we ought to give it a miss today, pal,' he said thoughtfully. 'Weather's building up. I don't like the looks of it at all.'

'Dunno, Bill. There's only today and tomorrow to go. We've never packed it in early before. Let's give it a go.'

The trip out to the pots was the roughest yet. The dogs stood together in the bows braced against the movement of the boat, noses lifted to the wind, drenched with salt spray. Once Skip almost lost his footing; after that the men called them back to the wheel-house. When they reached the floats which marked the position of the lobster pots, the boat hove to, bows pointing into the wind so that the long swell ran under her from stem to stern. The men began to pull in the pots. The first was empty, but they did not waste time in rebaiting it. It was clear from the ominous sky and the steepness of the sullen swell that there would be no fishing on the following day. The empty pot was flung into the body of the boat, and they started to haul in the rest. They worked quickly, and in silence, with the urgency of men who knew that with the waves running high and the wind rising their lives could soon be at stake.

All the pots were empty save the last in which there lay a beautiful blue-green lobster. As the wicker trap broke the surface of the water the creature waved an enormous claw. The dogs, who had clambered onto the gunwhales to watch, barked excitedly, and the dachshund, thrown off balance by a sudden pitch of the craft, fell into the sea. For a moment he floated motionless on the crest of a wave, then he vanished in a turmoil of broken water. Immediately the mongrel leaped overboard and swam with short, strong strokes towards his friend. Both men shouted, but he took no notice. Wave after wave seemed to engulf him, but as each crest passed his head could be seen bobbing in the trough. Somehow he found the dachshund and seized him by the loose skin at the back of his neck. He made his way towards the boat, but the seas were running so high that there was no way in which he could scramble aboard. He trod water alongside, his eyes begging for help; the dachshund kicked feebly. Skip's owner extended a boathook and tried to slip it under his dog's collar, while the other man leaned dangerously over the side trying to grasp the dachshund's tail. He managed to pull the dog from the mongrel's grip, and heaved him into the boat. Then he leaned down once more, intent on grabbing Skip. At that moment a huge roller lifted the bows in the air, the boat shuddered and plunged as the wave ploughed past, and the man was thrown overboard, plummeting head first into the water. He surfaced and tried to catch hold of the mongrel with one hand and the side of the boat with the other, while the younger man held out the boat hook. But another huge wave washed past, and man and dog disappeared.

The remaining fisherman quickly started his engine and began to circle the area. In the waste of grey, turbulent water there was nothing to be seen. He thought that the dog had probably been washed away in the wake of the waves, while his friend's thighboots had filled with water and taken him to the bottom. After a while, realizing that the search was fruitless, he headed for the port. Clouds lay like a vast, black pall over the sea.

Chapter Fifteen

The fisherman's body was washed up on the rocks below the headland, but the mongrel was never seen again. Skip's master took the dachshund to live with him, but from the outset there was no real friendship between them. The dog never felt really wanted, and deep in his heart the man blamed the animal for the deaths of his friend and Skip. During the wild winter months, when there was no work for the owners of small craft, man and dog spent most of their time indoors if the weather was bad, or mooching around the quays on finer days. At first they stayed together, but there was no communication between them – no thrown sticks, no pats on the head, no barkings, no lickings, no fun. Gradually they grew more and more apart, and in the end the man opened the door to let the dog out in the mornings and did not see him again until he came home for his evening meal. The arrangement suited them both very well.

That winter the dachshund explored every part of the village. He made friends with the children who played in the streets, he learned which butcher's shop was always good for a bone. He never went short of food at home, but like most dogs he was always ready for a little bit more. By the time spring came he had put on weight, but his shoulders and chest still bulged with hard muscle. He was no longer a young dog, but hard living had toughened him and kept him quick and agile. His coat, no longer groomed every day, grew coarse and rough, but he was exuberantly healthy. Friendly to all humans, he now deliberately avoided any close relationship and resisted with a sturdy independence any attempts to pet him.

In early spring when the small fishing boats put to sea again, he went out with one or other of the fishermen daily. His master did not seem to notice that he was aboard on the few occasions that the dog went with him. He appeared to blind himself to the lonely, brown body standing in the bows, perhaps because the sight brought back too many painful memories.

When summer came some of the men ceased fishing and spent their time on the less gruelling task of taking holiday makers for pleasure trips round the bay. The dachshund was popular with the visitors and often went with them: they called him 'Lucky'. He no longer went home at night but slept under an upturned boat on the beach or in a sea-front shelter. Food was no problem. The butcher gave him bones and scraps of meat, the holiday makers shared their ice creams and crisps with him, and there was always fresh fish to be found on the quays. His days were long and sunny and filled with interest.

At midsummer a party of school children came

to the village, engaged as part of their studies, in discovering the geography of the district. They quickly made friends with the dog and Lucky went with them on all their expeditions. At first he was frightened when he travelled on the school bus. He climbed aboard happily enough, but when the engine revved up and the vehicle began to move, he remembered the goods truck and scrabbled frantically at the door asking to go out. The children soothed him, so that he learned that a bus trip was something to be enjoyed. His relationship with them suited his mood perfectly: he was friends with everyone but had no master.

On the last day of their visit the boys and girls were scheduled to travel along the coast in one of the larger pleasure craft and to put ashore in a neighbouring town for tea. Lucky must, of course, go with them, so they made sure that he was aboard before they set out.

The day was calm and warm. The unwrinkled sea shone with diamonds of light, and the boat hissed gently through the water leaving a trail of white foam in its wake. The dog took up his usual position in the bows, his long nose lifted to the breeze. The children crowded the rails to watch the land as it disappeared from sight. A school of dolphins played through the water, leaping rhythmically above the surface only to dive back in a slow graceful curve. They followed the boat until it swung landwards and made for a harbour entrance.

The town where the children were to have tea

was the largest in the area. It was an industrial town and rail centre as well as a thriving port. From its harbour coasters plied their trade across the Channel to Continental ports as well as round the British Isles to the furthest tip of Scotland, to Wales and Ireland. The quay where the children landed was abustle with life: engines hooted, cranes clattered, men shouted and steamers whistled. The dog quivered with excitement – this was the sort of place where he had last seen the lad from the barge. All his past longings and affection for his young master came back with a rush.

As soon as they were ashore he ran off, dodging between trucks, avoiding kicks, pushing between legs; looking always for a familiar face, seeking a familiar smell. He ran along the wharves from boat to boat, yapping and sniffing and being cursed for his pains. Farther and farther along the quayside he ran, but nowhere could he find the barge. At last, realizing that he was hungry, he ran up a gangplank, following the warm smell of food. He found himself in the galley of a coaster where a cook's boy was ladling meat and gravy onto platters. The dog pawed at his legs and then sat up and begged. It was a trick that he did not often use, but it worked amazingly well. The boy filled a large dish with steaming food and placed it on the floor. He watched indulgently while the dog wolfed it, but when the meal was finished he took the animal back to the gangplank and shooed him ashore.

Chapter Sixteen

The dachshund tried several times to climb aboard the ship again, but always someone barred his way. At last he gave it up as a bad job and ran off along the quayside. It was now late evening and growing dark. Riding lights were being lit on the ships, and street lights shone in front of the warehouses which flanked the quays. Here and there a cat slunk stealthily from shadow to shadow, its prey the mice and rats which lived in the grain stores. The dog half-heartedly chased one scrawny black tom, but the animal reacted so viciously, spitting and yowling and lashing out with its needle-sharp claws that he quickly decided the game was not worth the candle.

He trotted the full length of the quays and back again. The dock workers had gone home leaving only a nightwatchman who took no notice of the animal. There was food to be had, but he was not hungry: there were sleeping-places to be found but he felt too unsettled to rest. There were so many smells that he recognized – the stench of train oil, the dusty smell of grain and the tang of the rotten weed which clung to the harbour walls. Surely somewhere here he would find the barge.

Someone had removed the gangplank from the ship where he had had his supper, but through the portholes he caught glimpses of light and heard human voices singing; he ran on, smelling over his own tracks. He paused at last at the foot of a lamp post where another dog had been and stood uncertainly in the circle of light wondering where to go next. The captain of the coaster which the dachshund had visited, a Dutchman, returning to his ship after an evening in a public house, saw the little brown dog standing in the pool of light and whistled to him. In his fuddled brain he confused the stranger with the memory of a dog which he had once had at home. 'Hullo, Fritz,' he called, and when the animal moved towards him, he slapped it heartily on the flanks saying, 'Huh, you very like Fritzy, but you Engleesh dog. You lost? You come with me.' His English was heavily accented, but the dog understood perfectly what he meant. He seemed friendly and he smelt kind so when he moved away the animal fell in at his heels. They came to an unsteady halt before the ship where the dachshund had fed. The man hallooed loudly and the gangplank was run out: man and dog went aboard. There was a lot of talk between the captain and another man who seemed to be advising that the dachshund should be put ashore, but finally the skipper stumped off shouting over his shoulder for the dog to follow him. They went to a comfortably furnished cabin where the man pulled off his shoes, flung himself on the bunk and fell asleep fully dressed. After a little while the dachshund jumped up and slept beside him.

The dog woke first. The boat was moving, and a greenish light came through the porthole. Spray slapped against the glass, and the air coming through the ventilator was cold and salty. The animal realized that they were at sea.

When the man awoke, he washed his face in cold water from the faucet over his wash basin, swilled out his mouth, shaved and replaced his rumpled uniform with a clean one. The dog followed him to the galley where they both ate. The cook said something to the captain which the dachshund could not understand, but which seemed to refer to him since both men looked at him and the skipper laughed loudly. 'It is surely this boat on which you must sail, my little one, is it not?' he chuckled. 'You have been here before.'

The ship went south-west down channel in heavy weather. The captain was pleased to see how well his new pet adapted himself to the conditions aboard. Always about the deck but never underfoot, the animal braced his legs against the seas like an old sailor. He was drenched by the spray which was flung over the sides, paddled knee deep through water which washed through the scuppers, but showed not the slightest sign of discomfort.

He spent all his time with the captain, eating in the galley when he ate, sleeping on his bunk, accompanying him on his duties about the ship. He liked and respected the man, but could not give him the trust and affection which makes the true bond between a human being and an animal. The Dutchman felt the barrier between them and could not understand what was wrong. He hoped that the dog would come closer to him as time went on.

After they had rounded Cape Finisterre, the wind dropped and the seas ran less heavily. The ship was going to ply its trade along the Portuguese and Spanish coasts and they sailed across the Bay of Biscay in an unusual calm. The seamen, glad to be free of the discomfort of wet clothes, revelled in the warmth of the sun. They played with the dog on deck, throwing balls for him to fetch, teasing him with pieces of rope. The captain watched indulgently.

When the ship docked at her first port of call the dog confidently expected to go ashore, but the captain called him harshly, 'Come,' and shut him in the cabin where he stayed the whole while the ship was at anchor. He found that by standing on a chest which was just below the porthole he could see through the glass, so he watched the cargo being unloaded and the new one being taken aboard. Along the quays men went to and fro about their work, but apart from the men from his own ship there was nowhere a friendly face. The place smelt strange too – hot and dusty, and the glare of the sunlight reflected from the water dazzled him. Often in the afternoon the cabin became unbearably hot and he lay on the chest, as near to the vent as possible, and panted. Relief only came when the sun sank and the long, dark evening shadows crept across the water, while the sea birds flew home to their nests. Fresh food and water was brought to him every day, but he missed the exercise which he normally took on deck. His eyes grew staring and his coat was lack-lustre.

For four nights the captain stayed ashore, then one bright afternoon he returned, and with him he brought a shoulder-blade of lamb with plenty of cooked meat still on it, and a rubber toy bone. The dog frisked round him and whimpered at the door, asking to go out, but it was clear that the man intended him to stay in the cabin for a while longer. His tail dragged on the ground and he looked the picture of dejection. Even the meaty bone could not make up for his loss of freedom.

On the next day they weighed anchor, and as soon as the ship was clear of the harbour the dachshund was allowed out on deck. Never had the air seemed so fresh and delicious: the boat was an exciting place and every corner had to be explored once again.

Chapter Seventeen

The weather continued fine and warm and the coaster moved through calm seas. The dog loved to roam the ship at night under the brilliance of a starlit sky, and in the day, in the heat of the afternoon, he sought a shady corner in which to sleep. Now and again the galley lad found a brush and groomed him so that his coat shone smooth and sleek.

The boat went south calling at several small ports to discharge or pick up cargo, but whether they were in the harbour for a day or a week the dog was always confined to the cabin. He grew to hate the sound of the anchor chain as it ran out and would bark furiously, jumping up and down with rage and excitement.

It was late summer when they passed through the Straits of Gibraltar and the dachshund crowded the rails with the men to watch the Rock slide by. On they went, up the Spanish coast, and the heat was intense. The days were heavy and humid and the nights brought no relief. They kept close to the coast and the heat came off the land like the glow from a furnace: it was too hot to sleep, too hot to play and almost too hot to eat. The cook's boy filled a shallow bowl with water and the dachshund wallowed in it, creeping out to lie in the shade while his coat steamed.

'Soon we go back to cooler places. We must turn round quickly here,' said the captain as once more he locked the dog into the cabin. The portholes were half open, the air vents were at their widest and there was a dish of iced water on the floor, but the dog still felt uncomfortably hot. He lay on the chest and gulped at the air which came through the various openings, but it was far too warm.

The quayside, which he could overlook, was unusually crowded, but the workmen moved slowly in the heat. He could see the captain in conversation with a man who was apparently the foreman in charge of the dockers who worked the quay. The captain was gesticulating, pointing at the coaster and thumping his fist into his palm, but the foreman was shaking his head. Then suddenly he clapped his hands on his thighs and laughed; the captain laughed too. The man went towards a warehouse and in a few moments a group of workmen came forward shepherded by the foreman. Another man moved the crane into position: the ship was winched forward and unloading began, with the captain himself speeding the work.

All was going well. Crates of apples were piled up on the wharf and the ship, lightened of the bulk of her cargo, was riding high when there was a sound of high pitched yelping, and a big dog, a crossbred alsatian, ran onto the quay. Foam was dripping from his jaws and his eyes were wild and staring. He looked bewildered and anxious: his coat was tufted and tangled and seemed as if it were wet. At the sound of his hysterical barking the dock hands had scattered, some into the warehouses, some aboard the ship. Someone hastily pulled up the gangway: only the crane-driver, high in his cab, was undisturbed.

The dachshund, forgetful of heat and discomfort, climbed to his feet to peer intently through the porthole. The captain stood alone on the quay, watching the dog which rushed up and down in a frenzy of madness. The man shouted to the ship an order that the gangplank be lowered, and the sound of his voice woke the animal to even wilder antics. It threw itself on the gound, snarling and biting at its tail, and dashed in circles round the quay. The man watched it warily, turning carefully so that he could always keep it in view. As soon as the gangway was in position, he leaped aboard, and the plank was quickly removed.

The dachshund had never seen a dog behave in such a strange fashion, but he had never seen a rabid animal before. His heart thumped in his chest, and he felt a queer mixture of fear and misery. When the mad dog faced the ship and barked its peculiar high pitched cry, he barked back, but this threw the animal into an even greater fit of hysteria. It contorted its body and slavered at the jaws and ran up and down the wharf without cease. The quayside was deserted, but the crane-driver was slowly manoeuvering his machine towards the animal with the obvious intention of either crushing it against a wall or of scooping it up, but before he could achieve either end, the captain of the coaster appeared on deck with a rifle in his hand. The dog was cornered by the crane and standing still for the moment. The man took careful aim and fired: the sick creature dropped dead as the sound of the shot echoed and echoed through the warehouses. The silence that followed was so complete that it seemed as if the world had died.

The dachshund stood motionless, hackles raised, only half understanding what had happened, then men ran out and removed the body. A faint smell of blood and death reached his nostrils and he flung back his head and howled. It was a long mournful howl and it expressed his puzzlement at what he had seen, his fear, his misery and his fright. He keened for himself and for the dead Alsatian; then he lay down with his head on his forepaws and shivered.

When the captain came into the cabin he petted the dog and said, 'There, now you know why I do not let you go ashore, huh?'

The next morning the coaster sailed westwards making its way back to the home waters of Northern Europe.

Chapter Eighteen

As the boat steamed north the temperature dropped rapidly. At morning and evening a haze hung over the sea, and during the day drifts of fleecy cloud obscured the sun. Everyone on board was grateful for the respite from the heat, and the crew went about their tasks with a greater alacrity. The dachshund chased seagulls about the deck and gobbled food in the galley. When they entered the English Channel, a stiff breeze came up from the west and a splatter of rain slanted over the ship. The sky grew dark and threatening, the horizon was a heavy, black line dividing the grey sea from the greyer sky; the waves which ran under the stern were white tipped.

The coaster sped on before the rising storm. She was not carrying much cargo so she rode lightly in the water, but because of this she was thrown this way and that as the sea boiled around her. Soon the wind reached gale force and the rain fell in torrents. The captain was constantly on the bridge watching his instruments, sending orders to the engine room; he looked tired and worried. The dachshund lay at his feet. Occasionally he sneezed.

The waves which brought about the disaster

seemed to come from nowhere. The first came racing up the Channel, towering many feet above the level of the sea, and broke over the stern in a welter of foam. The ship seemed to falter as she shook herself free of the water, but while she was still weighed down by the green flood which poured over her, another even greater wave flung itself upon her. She rolled broadside into the weather, wallowing and waterlogged, and it was clear that all chance of her survival had gone. Boats were quickly lowered in the comparatively calm water of her lee side, and the crew piled in. The captain snatched some papers from his cabin, seized the dog and tucked him under his arm, and abandoned ship.

The lifeboats pulled away quickly from the stricken vessel, but before they had covered any distance she vanished in a whirlpool of turbulent water.

The crew were stunned by what had happened; the disaster had overtaken them so suddenly. Only the dog was his usual self, wriggling and barking and playing in the water which sloshed about in the bilge of the boat. They set course for the French coast, but made little headway since the force of the gale was driving them up Channel. Ships passed on the horizon, and the shipwrecked men sent up flares, but no-one came to their assistance. There was ample food in the store which was kept aboard each lifeboat, so food was handed round and drinks were heated on the emergency stove. The men sang to keep their spirits up, and the dachshund wailed in unison. This amused the crew and together with the antics in which the dog engaged, provided them with something to laugh at and kept their minds off their plight. The more the men laughed, the more the animal clowned, and time passed quickly.

Even so, it was growing dark when they were at last picked up by a passing steamer. On board they were given dry clothes and hot food, and the dachshund was fed in the galley. Someone rubbed him down so that the worst of the salt was removed from his coat, and dry and fed he ran about the ship making friends with his rescuers. The shipwrecked crew were quick to say how he had entertained them on the lifeboat and kept their spirits up, and everyone made much of him. Unfortunately, he developed a heavy cold. His eyes ran and his muzzle was spotted with mucus, but the cook gave him hot milk with a dash of brandy, and he dozed groggily on his master's bunk. In the morning his cold had gone.

The steamer landed the crew in the great port of Amsterdam. The men were quickly discharged, but the captain was kept overnight in the city by the need to report on the loss of his vessel. The next day a vet examined the dachshund, innoculated him against rabies, and gave him a clean bill of health; in the early evening they set off on the electric train for the town near which the skipper lived. They travelled in the gathering dusk through the flat Dutch pastures and wide bulb fields. The dog looked out of the windows with interest. He was particularly excited when they ran alongside a dike and he could see the long straight water channel so like the waterways on which the barge had travelled. When darkness fell the lights of the distant city glowed against the sky.

They left the train at a town many miles from Amsterdam and walked in the moonlight through the deserted streets. The man was happy to be coming home and he hummed quietly to himself. The dog found it difficult to walk on dry land after so long at sea, but he splayed his legs and stumbled along beside his master. Soon he was trotting confidently, stopping to smell at every lamp post he passed.

The countryside beyond the town was wrapped in silence and shadow. A pale moon outlined the walls of the dikes and made each tree a black finger pointing at the sky. An owl floated down from a branch like a silver leaf falling . . .

The house to which they came was set by itself on the edge of a wide stretch of farmland. It stood square and snug in its own garden on a foundation which was slightly raised above the level of the surrounding ground. The captain's wife who came from her bed to greet them was loudly delighted with the dachshund and made a great fuss of him. Her husband explained how he had found the dog who had been his companion throughout the voyage.

They remained at the house for several weeks for the skipper had to wait until he was given another ship to command. During this time the dog happily roamed the garden and the wide pastures beside the house. There was no human company save the man and his wife, but he was well-fed and cosseted and had his freedom by day. At night he slept on a rug in the kitchen.

He loved to go out in the early morning when the polder was still bright with dew, to breathe in gulps of the air which came cold from the sea. He loved the spaciousness of the wide horizons and the vast sweep of the sky. Above all he loved to explore the reed-fringed dikes, lying for hours watching his lonely reflection in the water which flowed below.

Then, one morning, the captain came downstairs dressed in his sea-going uniform. He called the dog, and the woman hurried forward with a handful of the dachshund's favourite biscuits. She hugged him to her, then said her farewells to her husband, and watched from the window as they walked away towards the town.

Chapter Nineteen

In Amsterdam the captain received the command of a new ship. The dog bounded happily onto the vessel and watched the preparations for the voyage with knowledgeable interest. When they were under way, gently chugging through the waterway which connects the port with the North Sea, he nuzzled the skipper's leg and sighed a deep sigh of contentment. It was always good to be afloat.

Soon they left the muddy waters off the Dutch coast and were sailing past Belgian shores. They made landfall several times to load and unload cargo, crossed to the Channel Islands and came back to Cherbourg. Once again the dog was shut in the cabin while the ship was in port, but he no longer resented this. He realized that his imprisonment was only temporary, and the cabin was warm and snug while outside wind and rain slashed across the quayside and sometimes hail rattled against the porthole.

They left France in a raging gale, and set course for the West of England. Sullen white capped waves flung themselves against the bows, the bridge was hidden by a cloud of spray and the stern was a welter of wild water which drained away through the scuppers only to be replaced by another deluge as another wave hit them. The captain, dressed in sea boots and oilskins went about his duties; the dachshund stayed below.

The wind moderated as they approached the Cornish coast, and the frenzy of the waves gave way to an oily swell. They hove to in Carrick Roads in a comparative calm. When the Customs men came aboard for their routine inspection, the captain was reminded that although the dog had a certificate for an anti-rabies innoculation he must not go ashore in Britain without incurring a six month stay in quarantine. While in British waters he must not run loose on deck.

'It is a wise law,' said the man. He believed that quarantine for animals entering the country had kept England free of the dread disease of rabies, and he told them about the mad dog that he had shot on the Spanish coast. It would be a sad day if ever the disease came across the Channel and became an epidemic in this country – so many wild animals would have to be hunted down and slaughtered, so many cats and dogs would have to be destroyed. Certainly he would not dream of infringing the regulations. The dachshund would always be kept shut up on the ship while they were in port. 'But we haf much business in England,' he continued, 'so it maybe that he will become Engleesh dog. We shall be here more than six months since we do not return to Amsterdam until late summer.'

The Customs officers laughed and one went to

pull the dachshund's ears but was sternly reminded of the quarantine restrictions by his comrade.

During the winter months they moved from port to port around the British coasts. Westerly winds blew most of the time and the weather was wet and blustery, but in early spring the winds dropped. There were a few days on which a pale sun shone and the sea became a blue-green plain over which the cloud shadows played in ever changing patterns. Then a breeze sprang up from the northeast. It increased to gale force and the bitter cold of the Siberian wastes swept across Europe. The wind bit through the close, soft coat of the dachshund penetrating to his skin, and he shivered constantly. Snow began to fall so that the ship was mantled in whiteness. Even the salt sea spray froze in icicles on the masts and rigging.

After they had discharged cargo at the next port of call, they were unable to reload because the railway lines were blocked by snow so that the goods trucks could not come through. There were blocks of ice floating in the docks, and on the beaches the edges of the sea froze. A number of barges and coasters were tied up nearby, and their crews, muffled in sweaters and scarves, met on the quayside to talk about the delays which they were all having to endure. All nationalities exchanged greetings, speaking in broken English, using words from their native tongues and signs to make their meaning clear. They stamped the snow from their boots, lit each other's cigarettes, cursed the weather and blamed the government before returning to their various craft.

One morning the dachshund escaped from the cabin in which he was confined and huddled in the shelter of the wheel-house. Suddenly he heard a voice he knew. It was the lad from the barge, taller older, thicker set, but it was he; it *was* he. The dog rushed to the rails and barked delightedly, but the lad was walking away with a group of friends and did not hear. The dog barked and whined frenzedly until the men had moved out of sight.

The animal went nearly mad, rushing up and down the deck, throwing himself this way and that, tensing his body to spring onto the quayside, but the gap between the ship and the land was too wide. He thought wildly of leaping from the stern of the ship into the icy water and was preparing to do this when his master, roused by the turmoil, came and scolded him and carried him below. The man could not understand what had upset the dog nor why he remained restless and miserable, resisting caresses, refusing food in the following days. The animal spent his whole time peering out of the porthole of the cabin where his master confined him, whimpering quietly.

At last the railway lines were cleared so that the trains cme through, and the new cargo was loaded. The coaster set sail.

Chapter Twenty

Spring came almost overnight. The days grew brighter and warmer and the sea turned brown with the stain of silt, washed down by rivers swollen by melting snow. The coaster went from port to port, discharging, reloading, taking china clay from the West Country to the potteries of the north, carrying fish from the east coast to London, timber and wines to Scotland and cider to Liverpool. They visited the same places again and again so that the dog knew exactly where they were by the scents which came to him on the offshore breezes.

At each port of call he tried to break free, to hang about the deck, to watch, to listen for his former master, but without success.

It was summer when the captain told him that shortly they would return to Holland. The coaster needed to be repainted and certain repairs were necessary so they would be ashore for several weeks. It was a long while since he had been home and he looked forward to seeing his wife again.

At the next place they visited the captain went ashore with some papers and when he returned he brought a vet with him who examined the dog. The dachshund was surprised to be put on a lead and taken ashore. He did not realise that they had been in British waters now for more than six months and that the quarantine period was over.

It was good to feel soil under his feet again and to be able to trace the scents of other dogs. The captain grew impatient when he stopped to smell at a lamp post or wanted to investigate something in the gutter, and eventually he unclipped the lead so that the dog ran free. They went through the town, doing a little shopping, the dachshund trotting obediently at heel. When they returned to the ship the gangway was left down and the dog spent some time exploring the quays. After this it became the accepted thing for the dachshund to go ashore as he pleased, following his own pursuits throughout the day, but always returning to the ship at sundown in time for his evening meal.

Their last port before returning to Europe was an east coast harbour. It was a busy place and the coaster had to queue in mid-channel until a berth could be found for it at the wharf. The waterway was busy with craft of every kind from slender, white-sailed yachts to grimey, stubby colliers. Barges came and went, sailing from the quays inland up a broad river, dredgers constantly scoured deeper passages through the silt which the river brought down. They had not been here before, and the dog went ashore with a feeling of excitement. He quickly left the harbourside and ran through the town, but found little to interest him. A pleasure beach adjoined the harbour, and he spent the afternoon there begging scraps from holiday makers, tumbling and racing with other dogs, playing with children of whom he was extremely fond. When the heat of the day was passed and the long, evening shadows crept across the sands, the holiday makers packed their bags and went back to their lodgings. The dachshund was left alone with abandoned sandcastles, empty ice cream cartons, discarded chocolate wrappings and the cigarette stubs which littered the beach. It was long past the time at which he normally returned to the ship, but he was not hungry and felt in no hurry to go.

At last, after one final gallop along the waterline, and one last defiant bark at a loitering seagull, he went back to the quayside. Men were leaving their ships for an evening's entertainment ashore, lights were already lit at mastheads, the warehouses were closed and the dockers had gone home. A puddle of water reflected the light of the moon. . .

By the Customs House a knot of young men were talking together. The dog eyed them, sniffed, and then rushed forward wildly. It was *he*. It *was*. He could hardly believe his eyes and ears, but he knew that his nose could not deceive him. It *was* the lad from the barge, talking with a group of friends!

The young man turned round as the dog ran up and a look of amazement crossed his face: then he bent down and scooped the wriggling body into his arms. 'It's my Dachsie; it surely is my Dachsie,' he cried, ignoring the doubting remarks of his companions. 'I thought he had gone forever.'

The dog licked his face and squirmed with pleasure while the lad sat on a bollard and petted him. The other men drifted away but the man and his dog were so wrapped up in each other that they did not even notice.

Presently they set off along the quayside to where the barge was moored. The dog trotted and leaped beside his master.

The bargee and his wife were also delighted to see the dachshund again. The man told his son that this time they must take more care of the animal. 'First of all we must give him a real name so that he knows that he is special to us,' he cried. The young man, his arms full of wriggling dog, nodded agreement. 'What shall I call him?' the lad mused. 'A dachshund is a German breed of dog. Perhaps he should have a German name. I think I shall call him Hans.'

The dog knew that at last he really *belonged* to someone.